THL

THE DROWNING

BY HAMMOUR ZIADA
TRANSLATED BY PAUL G. STARKEY

Interlink Books

An imprint of Interlink Publishing Group, Inc.
Northampton Massachusetts

First published in 2022 by

Interlink Books
An imprint of Interlink Publishing Group, Inc.
46 Crosby Street, Northampton, MA 01060
www.interlinkbooks.com

Copyright © Hammour Ziada, 2019, 2022
Translation copyright © Paul G. Starkey, 2022
Originally published in Arabic in 2019 as *Al-Gharaq*, by El-Ain Publishing, Cairo, Egypt

Library of Congress Cataloging-in-Publication data:
ISBN-13: 978-1-62371-906-7

Printed and bound in the United States of America

To you… for sure

THE COUNTRY LOOKS as though it was made by accident, with no clear plan, and in a hurry.

And out of some unknown love, or as some kind of experiment, heaven had given it a river from paradise, and called it the Nile.

It rushes down from the highlands in the south to the lowlands in the north.

On either side of it there came first green, then desert. Raiders, occupiers, conquerors, the defeated, travelers, merchants, and armies arrived, but no one knows where they went.

A long time passed, and the inhabitants changed; their lives changed, but the Nile did not change.

The paradise river carried wooden boats, conquerors' barges, the corpses of the drowned, and the victims of massacres. Married couples, children after circumcision, and women after childbirth plunged into it.

The paradise river often flooded and killed.

The paradise river often dried up and destroyed.

But every time it went back to what it had been: a gentle river, coming from paradise.

What was it doing here? Nothing. It was just flowing languidly past the unmemorable village of Hajar Narti.

Embracing her like an absent lover, tightening its grip on her as she tries to flee, refusing to let her go.

Hajar Narti slopes down from the thirsty desert to the east, and the waters of the Nile block it to the west, to prevent it from escaping.

It bends gently over it but it is really harsh.

For it is from paradise.

Whatever comes from heaven has a reason, but we are too unimportant to comprehend its wisdom.

The wisdom is there. We do not know it, but we believe it.

Like light to a blind man. He has never seen it, and does not comprehend it, but he believes in it.

All we know is that there is the Nile, and that it has come from paradise. And that, starting from the month of May, it is flooded all summer long. Today it is flooded.

Now it is approaching Hajar Narti, carrying on its surface the remnants of a pool of gasoline from a steamship; some wood, eaten away by the water; an orange peel chucked away by some teenagers in a hiding place on the river; some shrubs that collapsed into it; bits of grass that at first resisted but were finally defeated by the current; the bloated corpse of a donkey; and what looks like the pages of an exercise book that some pupil had taken a dislike to and had fed it to the river.

'Abd al-Razeq was walking slowly along the riverbank, hands clasped behind his back, without a care in the world. He hummed a song by al-Na'am Adam: "You who forgot us, why did you forget us? You held my heart in trust. You who forgot us, why did you forget us?" His eyes followed the agricultural project channel. If he came across something in his way, he bent over and cleared it with a lump of earth. 'Abd al-Razeq was a dark-skinned man in a land where everyone was dark-skinned. He was short and his body was smooth, like that of a bygone wrestler. He raised his eyes to the Nile, noticed some reddish debris, and stopped to look more carefully. He didn't rush. It was some sort of fabric, no doubt about it. Red fabric—or perhaps white fabric embroidered with a lot of red, or possibly red with white patches on it.

He stepped out onto the jetty to get closer to the water and bent down, as if he was following a track in the current. When a wave struck the clump he was watching, he no longer had any doubts.

"Hey! Over here, everyone!" 'Abd al-Razeq shouted.

Nearby, a group of people were chatting together at Fayit Niddu's.

Fayit Niddu had a thatched-roofed shack at the jetty where she sold tea and coffee, and sometimes a little food, if the ferry was late.

Today Hajj Bashir was with her, along with al-Asghar al-Rashid's sister, Suleiman al-Hawati, and Ahmad Shigrib, the new medical assistant.

While 'Abd al-Razeq was shouting, Hajj Bashir was complaining that the ferry was late, for he had a lot of commitments. He started to spell out the things waiting for him, but Shigrib interrupted him to tell the crowd what he had heard a few minutes ago on the surgery radio: there had been a military takeover.

Hajj Bashir thumped the ground with his open fist, throwing up the soft soil. He coughed several times. "More soldiers?" he asked impatiently.

In the old days, Hajj Bashir had been a well-proportioned man, solidly built like fired mud brick. But for some months he had been losing weight, like a cow's teat sucked dry by a calf. He had a slight squint in one eye and a small beard tinged with gray. Although he was a year or two past fifty, he had never worked in his life—not a single day—but he explained his persistent weight loss over several months by saying, "Work and worry don't let a man put on weight." He was the grandson of a village chief, son of a local chief, and brother of the district sheikh. What need did the position to which the world had elevated him have of work? But he was always busy doing something; and today he was busy with a wedding. Even if he had nothing to occupy him in Hajar Narti or its neighborhood, he was always in demand to give evidence in the Dongola city court or the agricultural department in Al Goled, or on his way to mediate with the probate judge in Meroe. Thus, his opinion was always given a lot of weight.

He gave full vent to his annoyance. "This place has gone to the dogs," he said, "can you believe it?"

Shigrib, the only government employee, was more cautious. "Perhaps this time will be different," he said.

Fayit Niddu reminded him that it had only been six years since the children of Hajar Narti had shouted against the military in imitation of the demonstrators in the cities: "Back to your barracks, you insects!"

"Even the schoolgirls," she said. "They didn't know anything and they'd never worked. But they could shout and run!"

"This Sudan has a devil living in it!" said Suleiman al-Hawati with conviction.

As the thirty-one-year-old Rashid tried to interrupt the older people's conversation, they were shocked to hear 'Abd al-Razeq shouting. "There's a corpse in the river, everyone! Come on, let's get on with it, there's a corpse in the river!"

They left the shack, jumping between and over the palm trees, while others quickly emerged from the water channels blocked with straw that they had been unjamming. It was as though the earth had given birth to them. They were the color of the earth and their clothes were off-white, the color of gray birds. Dozens of people gathered together, shouting, "A corpse in the river! A corpse in the river!"

Without thinking, several jumped into Suleiman al-Hawati's boat, the only one tied up on the riverbank. The boat shook in protest and leaned to one side, throwing several men out. In fact, it was just an iron barrel that had been cut in two from top to bottom, and with a little smithy work, one half had been turned into a boat.

Hajj Bashir stood giving orders. He had a powerful voice, impossible to disobey.

"Suleiman, Rashid, Shigrib, and 'Abd al-Razeq no one else in the boat!"

A few people protested quietly but Rashid hurried to explain his brother's decision.

"Suleiman knows his boat and 'Abd al-Razeq has the best eyes and saw the corpse, so he's the best one to track it down. And Shigrib is a medical assistant and can offer help!"

He was surrounded by questioning looks. "And I will try to grab the corpse," he went on, with some embarrassment. "Though if there's someone better, that's fine."

The protestors grudgingly retreated, for in the end, "The good word plucks the lion's moustache," as they say in those parts.

The boat set off with its cargo and slowly moved further away. When a wave would push against it, Suleiman would do the same, like a child of the Nile, or like the mythical horses of Dongola. Whenever the water threatened to get the better of him, he won the struggle in the end. The folk on the riverbank shouted, encouraged, and directed. Then 'Abd al-Razeq spotted the corpse. It was surrounded by straw and dry branches, which had no doubt accompanied it on its long voyage down the Nile. The corpse was face down. "A woman!" said Suleiman confidently.

Shigrib, who was new to this style of life, didn't understand. "A man's corpse floats on its back, face upward," explained 'Abd al-Razeq, bending toward him. "But a woman, being modest by nature, floats face down."

"God be praised!" said Rashid, and Suleiman confirmed it. "I've seen hundreds of drownings. A woman's face is always down. Your Lord protects the woman even in death."

As the boat drew closer, the corpse could be seen more clearly. It was floating on its face, like an inflated lump of dough. The head was bald, except for a few hairs. It was a white, waxen color, with blue veins—as if injected with indigo dye—and spots of blood were visible underneath the skin.

But Ahmad Shigrib, the new medical assistant at the Hajar Narti surgery, was now suffering from something else. As the boat got closer to the corpse, they were hit by the smell. It wasn't a penetrating smell, but it was a heavy smell. It had a presence.

Can you smell it?

The smell of death, acquired when the first dead body rotted on top of the earth, before the crow taught us to rot beneath the earth. The smell of dead bodies the crow harvested everywhere. It was not the smell of embalming, not the smell of death in a winding-sheet. The smell of raw, virgin death. Death with no preparation, no loved ones, and no tears, as if it was just death.

It was a heavy smell, it left a taste in the mouth.

Can you taste it?

He felt it as a burning in his eyes.

Has it made you cry?

As if death itself had died and been left to rot beneath the sun for a thousand, thousand years.

While Rashid was unravelling a cloth bandage to secure the hand of the corpse, Ahmad Shigrib had swallowed the smell of death so he no longer had space for life inside him.

Without being aware of it, and with no prior warning, Shigrib leaned over the side of the boat and emptied his stomach.

"You idiot, not over the corpse, you idiot!" shouted Suleiman al-Hawati.

The state of the corpse did not allow it to be taken out of the river. "It will disintegrate if we try to retrieve it," said Suleiman al-Hawati.

They secured the corpse to the river bank beside the boat, and helped each other up. Then they gathered in Fayit Niddu's shack.

Ahmad Shigrib ran to the project's irrigation pump, pursued by the smell, which choked him, filling every part of his being. He put his head under the spouting water.

In the other direction, they could hear the clanking of the ferry, as it carried across the passengers at midday.

Hajj Bashir stood there, giving instructions. He coughed for a few moments, then sent a group to the village mosque to announce the news there. He ordered another group to head for the village of Quraysh Baba to the south to tell them that a drowned woman had been retrieved. If it wasn't one of theirs, a group would go south from Quraysh Baba to inform the villages further upstream. "Come on, everyone, get moving, you and him!" he shouted, to hurry up their departure.

The groups split up quickly. "How many days will the corpse last?" Hajj Bashir asked Suleiman al-Hawati.

"Two days at most."

"Okay," he said, counting on his fingers, "today's Sunday, Monday,

Tuesday. If her family hasn't appeared by then, we'll bury her after the noon prayer."

Approval could be heard all around from the small group.

Hajj Bashir performed his ablutions with a little water in Fayit Niddu's shack. The woman complained but he ignored her. Her mother, and her family before her, had belonged to Hajj Bashir's family. The abolition of slavery had not made her free; she was just no longer an official slave.

Hajj Bashir used what little water the shack had then advised all those who were with him to perform their ablutions. "Whoever carries a corpse should perform their ablutions, and whoever washes it must wash themselves; this is the law," he told them.

'Abd al-Razeq, the irrigation channel watchman, laughed. "The project water is here, and the Nile is there. Are you supposed to perform your ablutions with poor Fayit Niddu's water?"

Fayit Niddu pulled her tall, muscular body up and called her daughter. "Abir, come here, to fill up the water. Your uncle Bashir hasn't left us any!" Then she turned to 'Abd al-Razeq, "No one treats us properly here except you!"

Abir, Fayit Niddu's daughter, went into the shack, and the place acquired a smell, like the smell of guava leaves under the rain.

She was a thin girl, dark as black magic, with youthful legs that glittered like the moon over the Nile. Her breasts were like unripe lemons, scarcely concealed by her young girl's clothes.

"There is no power and no might save with God!" whispered Hajj Bashir, as she bent down to pour the water. Suleiman al-Hawati smiled and took a deep breath, wishing he could swallow the young girl with it. The eyes of the others lit up, as if to acknowledge that she was now walking inside their veins. Rashid leaped out, looking at Ahmad Shigrib trying to wash the smell of death from himself until he almost flayed his skin.

As Abir left her shack, Rashid was almost struck blind. The girl was not beautiful, but she was inviting, like the promise of health to a sick man. He made her stop for no reason.

"Does the smell of the corpse disturb you?" he asked her.

She shrugged her shoulders and licked her lips nonchalantly. As she tried to slip away, he grabbed her wrist. "You've grown up, Abir!"

She looked at him with dead eyes, as if she was a guava pecked by a bird. Her smell was sweet and tempting, her hair unkempt and dusty, like a child's.

He heard the sound of the ferry and the muttering of his brother Bashir behind him. As he let go her wrist, she flew off like a dove. Hajj Bashir thumped his brother on his back. "The ferry's arrived," he said. "Come on, let's get back to work. The moulid is in a few days, and the wedding as well. There's a lot to be done. No more bad behavior!"

He didn't hang about. His brother treated him like a child, although he was a man in his thirties. And he in turn loved him as a child loves his father, for he had known no father but his two brothers.

He went down behind him to the ferry, past the departing groups of *ghajar*[*].

Hajj Bashir spoke harshly to the ghajar. "Have you come back again? Won't you give us a break?"

"Be kind, Hajj Bashir. We are God's guests!" one of them replied in a thick, drawn-out voice.

The ferry captain scolded them. "You don't know God!" he laughed.

"God forgive you!" replied a ghajari woman in the same husky, drawn-out voice.

Rashid passed them as they left the ferry and he embarked, but he scarcely noticed them. Abir, Fayit Niddu's daughter, was embarking with him, arousing his desire.

<small>*   Most dictionaries define the Arabic word *ghajar* as traveling people who live in caravans or wandering from one place to another, similar to the Roma. The Arabic term *ghajar* / *ghajari* has been retained in the translation in preference to gypsy / gypsies, which is regarded as pejorative in some contexts.</small>

AHMAD SHIGRIB HAD never before washed so thoroughly as he did that day. He wished he could put his fingers into his lungs to pluck out the smell.

After more than an hour, he felt relaxed. The water in the pump had begun to dry up, in preparation for stopping. The ferry had gone and come back twice, depositing its loads of passengers and taking on board others. Dozens of people had come from the village to see the corpse in its place under the river bank, tied in a cloth garment, lifted by one wave then lowered by the next. The onlookers exchanged predictions about which village it was from. From Quraysh Baba or Kallero, Sarwa or al-Konj.

Someone said a girl had run away from Quraysh Baba several weeks ago, but the corpse looked fresh. "This is a three-day old corpse," Suleiman al-Hawati said confidently. "When someone drowns, chains come out of their nose to hold them to the bottom for three days, then they are released. This is a corpse that drowned not more than three days ago."

Ahmad Shigrib put on his damp clothes and went off. Someone who was returning called him to jump on behind him on the donkey. But he felt dizzy and declined.

"I'll go on foot. I'll take the shortcut across Muhammad Said's land and from there home across the channel."

"The donkey will be more comfortable for you, man!"

"I can't do that. I've got a stomachache. If I ride, I'll feel nauseous, I'm bound to."

He heard people laughing, making fun of his delicate nature. A group of donkey riders passed him and he turned left to enter the district sheikh Muhammad Said's land.

Unlike everyone else in the small village, he wore trousers of white material and a short-sleeved shirt of the same color. It was his official uniform, as a medical assistant responsible for the village clinic—a small room standing on the road near the district sheikh's house, with bare shelves except for some tranquilizers, a stethoscope, and a single syringe, which he sterilized whenever he needed it.

He was tall and thin, with a slightly stooped back, as if he liked to look at the ground when he walked.

He walked on a few paces, until the palm trees shaded him. He stopped under one of them, bent down, then belched loudly. As the smell pursued him, his saliva flowed, though his stomach wouldn't bring anything up. He blew his nose hard, wiped his hand on the ground, then sat down. The place was extremely quiet; silent, except for birds chirping in the distance, the braying of a donkey somewhere or other, and a breeze whispering between the palm leaves. A secluded space, with nothing but shade.

Muhammad Said was the biggest landowner in the village, followed by his two brothers, Hajj Bashir and al-Rashid, then by the land belonging to the al-Badri children, one of whom Hajj Bashir had married. Despite all that had happened in the past, he was still in dispute with them over his inheritance. Perhaps if the problem had been settled years ago, Hajj Bashir would have become the biggest landowner in the village. But who knows what will happen tomorrow?

Ahmad Shigrib heard a rustle from someone moving nearby and prepared to get up. He expected Muhammad Said to appear on his enormous white male donkey, with his shoulder-wrap and stick. But instead of the proud old man, Abir appeared, with some unripe doum fruits gathered in her *tobe*.

She stood there, at a distance from him, saying nothing.

Did Ahmad Shigrib remember ever hearing her voice?

He had seen her for the first time a year and a half before, in his first days in the village. She was dancing at Hajj Bashir's son's circumcision party—her "uncle Bashir," as the new conventions of slavery required that he be known.

She was dancing like a willow branch, swaying in the wind. Whenever she leaned her thin body—not a wrinkle or bump to be seen—the crowd heaved and the youths let out a whistle. There was something of the Night of Power about her. You sensed it rather than saw it. You knew it, though your hands did not possess it. It was there, but what was it?

Now she was standing silently in front of him; submissive as a small bird in the hands of a child.

She didn't move past him.

She wasn't stealing anything, to feel she had been exposed. He hadn't spoken to her, to justify her staying.

She simply stood.

He looked at her carefully with the eye of a trained medical assistant, who had studied for several months, and made a bet with himself that she was no more than thirteen years old. But she possessed the femininity of thirteen women.

He beckoned to her and she came closer, moving toward him without a word. When only a few paces remained between them, the edge of her *tobe* in which she had gathered the unripe doum came loose and fruit scattered everywhere.

She didn't care. She walked toward him in silence until she disappeared in him.

***

When he had finished, Ahmad Shigrib slipped away, walking between the palm trees and contentment.

Abir had washed from him the smell of death and anointed him with life.

As he neared the main channel, he was met by the dust of some new arrivals, coming like clouds before rain. Silent on their donkeys, scattering the fine dust like disturbed smoke.

One of them threw him a greeting. He recognized among them some faces from the village of Quraysh Baba.

There were nine of them in their white jilbabs, on top of which perched their turbans and their worry. They had received news of the corpse in the river and had come to check. They passed the dry part of the main channel until they reached the muddy area, soaked from the last of the pump water. They branched off onto a narrow path between the palm trees. Whenever they passed a group of farmers they gave them a lukewarm greeting, which the farmers stopped to return with enthusiasm, then followed it cheerfully with: "All well, God willing!" A reassurance in which there was no certainty, but it was the custom.

They remained edgy until they reached Fayit Niddu's shack.

It was afternoon, and the weather was a bright yellow color. They leaped from the backs of their donkeys, quickly tethered them, and were met by a crowd of people on foot.

Greetings and embraces, followed by a cheerful, "All well, everyone! All well, God willing!"

One of the new arrivals—a fat, swarthy sheikh—took hold of 'Abd al-Razeq's arm and the two of them walked down to the riverbank, followed by a third man. Those waiting exchanged bags of tobacco soaked with herbs.

"Take this. It's El Fashir tobacco."

"My bag is new. I bought it today."

One of them opened his small bag and smelled it deeply. Then he made a little into a ball and buried it behind his lip.

"How is everyone? Well?"

"Well, praise be to God!"

"Have you heard about the coup?"

"Everything is in turmoil."

"Is it summer or hell this year?"

As they made conversation, Fayit Niddu brought water and coffee out to them, and they sat down under a nearby tree. "Come into the shade, everyone!" They thanked her, took the coffee, and someone asked for tea.

"This time the soldiers will rule till doomsday!"

"So long as they give us petrol, that's fine!"

"How are your fava beans this year?"

They made some unintelligible noises, which perhaps meant "Praise be to God" or "Okay."

"So long as they give us petrol, everything will be fine."

Then a turban appeared from below the riverbank, followed almost immediately by 'Abd al-Razeq, who was pulling the man wearing the turban. With some difficulty, he helped him up and the pair straightened themselves up. "It's all okay," people muttered to one another. As the fat sheikh clapped his hands together to shake off the dust, the third man who had gone down appeared behind them.

"It's not her."

Fayit Niddu smiled. "Praise be to God!"

No one asked about their missing girl or when and how she had gone missing. Perhaps the question would open a wound of honor or provoke an inappropriate curiosity.

One of the nine newcomers asked, to check, "Are you sure?"

"Quite sure. It's not her."

The corpse in the river wasn't the girl from Quraysh Baba. And that was that. Delegations from the other villages would come to see for themselves.

They gathered again beneath the tree. Fayit Niddu hurried to her shack, calling Abir, but the girl didn't appear. Many people were disappointed.

"How is everyone? Okay?"

"Fine, praise be to God. How are you?"

"Things are okay."

They sipped their coffee slowly. "Sugar, woman!" someone called to Fayit Niddu, "Your coffee is bitter!"

"My coffee is perfect," she replied from inside her shack. "It's your tongue that's bitter!"

They laughed, and someone muttered, "It's the coffee that lost the post of 'umda." More laughter.

The fat, swarthy sheikh shuffled forward to assume his role as chair of the gathering. "The story of the coffee that lost the post of 'umda is amazing!" he said to no one in particular.

They all knew it. They smiled, but raised no objections.

"They say that in the days of the British the regional ma'mur would go around the villages by boat, meet the 'umdas at the quayside, hear their problems, and solve them."

"The days of Jackson Pasha," commented 'Abd al-Razeq. "The country was in good shape, by God, when the British were here."

The sheikh took no notice of him and went on. "They say that, on his way to the quay, the 'umda met a group drinking coffee. They invited him to join them, but he made his apologies, so that he could meet the ma'mur. But when he smelled the aroma of the coffee, the man couldn't stand it. He got down from his donkey and said, 'Okay, then, a cup of coffee!'"

As the laughter grew louder, in anticipation of what would follow, Fayit Niddu brought the sugar, with more coffee and tea.

"Cup after cup of delectable coffee. When the British ma'mur's ship arrived and he didn't find the 'umda, he was angry. Now, the British are practical people; they don't go in for playing about with no discipline. So they issued a decree to remove the 'umda and appoint one of those present in his place!"

They burst into more laughter.

"The post of 'umda disappeared."

"He went with the coffee, much good may it do him!"

They remembered the story well. They knew all the stories, but they enjoyed them every time.

"That was 'umda Sarwat Allah, may God have mercy on him. 'Umda Barir."

"No, man. That was 'Umda Umkabul."

"It didn't happen here, people. They say it happened in Jaaliin country in Shendi."

"No, by God, it happened in Tangasi."

The fat sheikh assumed the leadership of the gathering once again. "God knows where it happened. But they say it happened."

They told all sorts of stories, stories with nothing new in them. They laughed, and people added to others' stories, as they enjoyed themselves.

When the sun was about to set, they stood up.

"Now what's the plan?"

Some people invited others to go home with them, but they excused themselves. Invitations and excuses were exchanged until they grew tired.

"With us on Friday, God willing, at 'Abd al-Hafez's wedding?"

"In sha' Allah."

"We must. The henna ceremony is tomorrow. And the contract ceremony is on Friday in the mosque."

"We'll be there if the Lord allows it!"

"Tell everyone!"

"The bill for the coffee and tea!"

More than one person swore and declined the invitation. Someone swore to divorce his wife. Impossible.

They leaped onto their donkeys and pushed them to start them on the way back, moving off as clouds move after rain. The sun sighed over its last glow and prepared to sink into the sunset. The earth was suffused with the smell of damp clover.

"Someone needs to spend the night here to guard the corpse."

They discussed the choice, as Fayit Niddu collected her things and turned off the light. Someone paid for what the guests had drunk. She called Abir loudly one last time. But the girl didn't oblige the lustful men.

"Hajj Bashir and Rashid haven't returned yet," said Suleiman al-Hawati. "I'll wait for them in my boat. Maybe all night."

Someone promised to come to him with the dawn prayer.

"Okay. I'll wait until dawn, then you take my place."

Fayit Niddu picked up her things and the herdsmen loaded their clover onto the backs of the donkeys. They moved along the road toward the village, some riding, some on foot, leaving Suleiman al-Hawati with the tail ends of their voices and the clatter of their departure.

He headed for the project channel, where a pool of water remained after the irrigation machine had stopped. He washed in it, took off his sandals and turned toward the east, raised his hands to recite "Allah akbar," and the sunset call to prayer came to him from the darkness of the village in the distance.

It was during his second prostration that he became aware of someone approaching. Out of the corner of his eye, he caught sight of a woman's *tobe*. He didn't think twice. The girl's mother had come.

Twenty-eight years.

Since 1941, as the official records stated. Or, as the oral history of the village had it, since the year of the marriage of Hajj Bashir to Sukaina bint al-Badri. Every village in the district knew Fatima, the girl's mother. She had never failed to turn up, even once.

The news reached her when it reached her. People had stopped asking how. She came wrapped in her *tobe*. She inspected the drowned corpse and examined it in case it was Su'ad.

Twenty-eight years.

None of the corpses in the river was that of Su'ad, but Fatima did not stop. She came every time. She stayed where the corpse was for weeks, sometimes for months. Waiting.

They say that the River Nile, when it spits out a corpse, follows it with two older corpses it had previously held on to.

Fatima would come and wait. Sometimes the River Nile would confirm the rumor, and spit out some old drowned bodies, which the people and the waves of the river had forgotten. Fatima would examine what the Nile had given up but did not find Su'ad.

Twenty-eight years.

People had died and people had been born. Palm trees had been planted and uprooted. The flood had destroyed gardens and people had planted others. But Fatima never despaired.

Twenty-eight years.

Fatima came this time as she had always done. She passed by Suleiman al-Hawati as if she couldn't see him. Silent, as if her tears had sewn her lips shut. He noticed her out of the corner of his eye standing on the path, looking at the path leading down.

Then she cautiously descended toward where the corpse was secured. In the hope that it might be Su'ad.

Fayit Niddu went into her house with the darkness, put down what she was carrying, and walked steadily towards her old lamp.

She could see nothing but she knew the place of everything. She grasped the lamp, and shook it to check it. It was full of white kerosene. She stretched out her hand and picked up a box of matches. The match caught fire and the red light exploded in the darkness. She lifted the glass of the lamp and touched the wick with the burning wood. Light filled the one remaining room. On the one bed at the edge of the room she saw Abir, sitting with her legs drawn up to her chest, her chin resting on her knees.

She wasn't doing anything. She was just there.

"Won't you stop these devilish deeds, girl?"

Abir didn't answer. Silence was her usual answer to any words directed at her. Silence was her preferred form of gossip.

Fayit Niddu pointed to her things that she had brought back with her. "Wash the cups, and arrange the equipment," she told the girl.

Abir slipped off the bed, and spread out the cups, with the tray and the coffee machine. She put aside the boxes holding the tea, coffee, and sugar, grabbed a bowl and a jerry can full of water, and sat down.

Fayit Niddu looked at her.

Her wealth, that she had taken from the world.

Fayit Niddu was still in her mid-forties but she knew that her life had ended before it had started, and she dreamed of a different life for Abir. From the first moment she had known she was pregnant she had prayed to God and the saints and shaykhs, to anyone with any power, to give her a daughter.

And so it was.

Abir had no official father. But Fayit Niddu knew and the whole village knew.

It was a summer night like this one, and Hajar Narti was bathed in moonlight. The guests in the sitting room of Muhammad Said's house, the district sheikh, were making a lot of noise. The regional judge was a guest of the village, so Muhammad Said had slaughtered some animals and sent people to buy imported wine. Sherry was being served beside local arak. The sitting room was too small for all the lamps and wines and meats and faces of the district, from Hajar Narti and the villages adjoining it to the district boundary.

Most of the conversation was about politics. It was the year of independence. The occupiers had left and the country had reverted to its people. The regional judge had stressed the ability of Colonel Ismail al-Azhari to rule and administer better than the British had done. Those present confirmed that the agreement of Sayyid Ali al-Mirghani, descendant of the Prophet, may God be pleased with him and grant him peace, and 'Abd al-Rahman al-Mahdi ibn al-Imam al-Mahdi, on whom be peace, would provide the necessary stability. But Muhammad Said al-Sheikh, driven by the effect of the drink, and enthused by his religious fanaticism, shouted, "There is no one of importance in this country except for Sayyid 'Ali al-Azhari." His assertion that the position of al-Mirghani was more important than the others embarrassed some of those present, some of whom started to mutter about the importance of 'Abd al-Rahman al-Mahdi, the father of nationalism. The gathering almost descended into disarray, and would have done, had not one of the intellectuals persuaded somebody to sing. From nowhere, a tanbur appeared; the performer took hold of it, tuned it slightly, then started to sing.

Politics fell silent, and the drunken assembly bowed their heads to listen.

In the silence of the village, the houses heard the song. Those still awake in their homes came out into their yards. Fayit Niddu heard the singing like magic with the women in the district sheikh's kitchen. And between the noise of the servants and the sweetness of the singing in came 'Abd al-Hafez.

Eleven women were preparing the food and drink in military harmony led by Hajja Radiya, the mistress of the house and of the village. As 'Abd al-Hafez came in, some raised the *tobes* covering their heads while others winked at each other.

The women thought he had come to ask for more food for the guests. But he stood there, talking about unconnected things in a confused way. He secretly made a sign to Fayit Niddu then left.

She hesitated a little before she stood up. She was tall and swarthy, her hair short and rough. But her face was sweet and enticing, as if created from pure wine. She asked permission to leave from the sheikh's wife, Radiya.

"Where are you going?"

She stammered and said something about fetching more firewood. But malicious laughter from some of the women put an end to her explanation. "Let her go," one of them said to Radiya.

Radiya looked at her suspiciously and at the women who were laughing and winking at each other, then said, "No."

Radiya—the woman that hated servants, slave-girls, and "rudeness"—almost lost her cool. But Sukaina bint al-Badri spoke out against her sister-in-law. "Let her go, Hajja!"

Fayit Niddu stood at the door of the kitchen, awaiting a reply. Even the fire under the utensils stretched out its flame in expectation. The women held their breath.

No woman in the village would dare to criticize what Hajja Radiya, the wife and cousin of the district sheikh, said. Her uncle was 'umda and her grandfather had been 'umda as well. The woman, who had inherited distinction even before her parents married, had a filthy, stormy temper from which no one was safe, even Muhammad Said al-Sheikh.

But Radiya's affection for her sister-in-law made the storm pass.

"Who is like you, Sukaina?" asked the district sheikh's wife fondly. "If every woman was like you and every man like Bashir, life would be sweet!"

The smile of satisfaction on the lips of Sukaina was a sign to Fayit Niddu to leave. She hurried away without turning back before the old woman could stop her.

Behind her, the women exchanged congratulations on the journey of Bashir and Sukaina, and refrained from cursing 'Abd al-Hafez as a mark of respect for his sister.

❦

It was a summer evening like this one. The villagers could hear the guests in Sheikh Muhammad Said's guest room and the voice of the singer calling to his beloved who had sailed away by boat.

Behind the kitchen stood al-Hafez wad al-Badri, waiting.

He put his hand on Fayit Niddu's arm and pulled her behind him. "I can't be too long!" she whispered to him.

He was tipsy, smelled of wine, and could hardly walk straight. "No problem, no problem," he replied to her.

He leaned her back against a wall. He lifted her *tobe*, and as he touched her naked thigh with his rough hands, she saw him in the light of the moon.

That night gave her Abir.

Her treasure, that took her from the world.

❦

Fayit Niddu asked her daughter if she had heard anything about the drowned girl.

Abir shook her head.

"I feel for her mother," Fayit Niddu replied. "A group came from Quraysh Baba. But she was not their daughter. Did you know the girl of theirs that ran away?"

Abir nodded her head.

Her mother spurred her on to speak, and her voice came out like a crawling child, as though she were asking rather than answering. "She was with me in school. Her name is Buthayna. Her father used to beat her; her brothers beat her, and the teachers beat her."

Her mother's heart boiled over, and Fayit Niddu shouted, "May God beat their hearts!"

"She slept a lot. She slept everywhere, and she slept during class. She was stupid. But she was waiting to marry her cousin so he could save her from school."

"She wasn't clever like you."

Abir answered with silence.

"The Lord is all-powerful, Abir, I'll see you as a doctor."

Abir looked at her mother. The pair were surrounded by oppression in the dark room. "No one knows the future except God," said Fayit Niddu. "And Hajja Radiya may get angry but she also quickly calms down. To be off school for a year is nothing."

Abir shrugged her shoulders as if she didn't care.

"If only Sukaina bint al-Badri were alive!" muttered Fayit Niddu.

"I don't remember her."

Fayit Niddu sighed. "She was the most beautiful woman anyone set eyes on. She was the sweetest person to walk on the earth."

Abir knew that Sukaina bint al-Badri was the person who named her. She imagined that if it hadn't been for Sukaina she would have remained an unknown creature without a name. But she hadn't seen her. She had only heard the story of her good life, which had come in installments, and with some caution, so as not to uncover the sorrow of Hajj Bashir or disturb Nur al-Sham.

With some difficulty, as if it was a dream, she recalled Shaykh Bashir shouting. He had his turban tied around his waist as he writhed on the ground. The village was wailing, and she could even hear the walls crying. She was a young child and ran and hid in her weeping mother's lap.

She didn't recall Sukaina bint al-Badri. But she remembered the tears and knew the pain.

People often repeated the expression: "If you haven't seen Sukaina bint al-Badri you haven't seen beauty." Indeed, when she was a child, they called her "Ma sha' Allah," so often did people who saw her say it.

Sukaina was the youngest daughter of Hajj Hussein al-Badri. But she was also the daughter of the full moon, of perfect beauty, and outstanding gentleness. She walked and the sand would trill under her childish feet; she whistled and the Nile would rejoice; she laughed and the palm trees would dance.

She was the first girl whose mother refused to scratch marks on her cheeks. Her face was smooth as a mango.

Neither the Nile nor the desert on either side of it had known a girl like her. She was spoiled by the whole of Hajar Narti. It was said that she was the first girl to wear leather sandals, which her uncle sent her from the capital. A group of women came to see the gift. When the girl put her pretty feet inside them, they were like the feet of a dove, with the same impression on the ground. "Ma sha' Allah," cried everyone who was there.

Sukaina walked in her sandals for months. When people praised something they said, "This is like Bint al-Badri's sandals!"

Every day that passed, she became more beautiful. When she awoke in the morning it was as if her beauty of the previous day had been exchanged for a sweetness no eye had yet seen.

Then what always comes to girls came to her. She was eleven or twelve years old, an age when men who desired her would not hold back.

She was the first person to be sought as a bride by one of her aunts, who wanted her for one of her children. Then the suitors increased in number. A poet who passed through the village one day (some people said he had seen her; others said he'd only heard about her) wrote a song about her beauty: "The fire in my heart has been set ablaze by Sukaina." And through his words news of her beauty reached villages in furthest Dongola to the north and to the borders of the Rabatab country to the south.

When Mahjoub, the only driver in the area, chose to write that line of poetry on the back of the long-distance bus, news of Bint al-Badri's beauty reached Omdurman. When the bus returned from one of its trips to Omdurman, a poem appeared, no one knew who'd written it:

> Come on, Mahjoub, get up and drive
> Leave Omdurman, hurry up and get going
> Let's see the beautiful woman of taste
> That all poetry falls short of describing.

Her uncle came that day, angry as the habub wind, his face black with fury. He blew his nose as if he was driving the devils from inside him, as he looked for his brother on his farmland. When he enquired of the farmers they answered him fearfully. The evil in the man's looks was frightening. They showed him the way and he went away, angry as he had come, and entered his brother's house without a greeting.

"Hajj, I cannot keep quiet any longer."

Her father, Hussein al-Badri, was a gentle, patient man. "Peace upon you too," he responded, trying to calm the situation. "Have you broken your fast?"

"What people are saying has left me with no appetite."

"People never stop talking," he replied politely. "Thank God for a good life."

"People's gossip is harmful. If they say something good, it attracts the evil eye, and if they say something bad, there's a scandal."

They were in the guest room of Hajj Hussein al-Badri's house, a long room built of mud brick with a straw mat on the floor. The two brothers sat close together. The sun fell on their faces through four windows, an open door, and cracks in the roof. If it hadn't been for the anger of one and the calm of the other, they would have looked alike.

"What's Sukaina done wrong?"

"And what have we done wrong that people are talking about us?"

"So what's to be done?"

"We'll marry her off."

Hajj Hussein was struck dumb. Sukaina was only fifteen and he had refused the proposal of marriage conveyed by his sister, as well as an administrative officer, the 'umda of Sarwa, the 'umda of Sarwa's nephew, and whole groups of people from Hajar Narti, some of whom he remembered and some of whom he had forgotten. Merchants, farmers, efendis from the village living in the capital, relatives and strangers, old men and men at the peak of their powers.

Whenever someone smiled at him in a gathering, he thought he must be seeking his daughter in marriage. Whenever he met a scowl that he suspected might be a suitor, he turned him away and forgot him.

"The girl's not ready for that!"

The man jumped up as though stung.

"Our girls have been married several years younger than she is. Her sisters were married several years younger than she is. My daughters were married several years younger than she is."

"Not all girls are the same!"

"All girls are the same, and all men's tongues are evil. If your intention is to cause a scandal among us, say so!"

"May God not bring a scandal!"

"Then don't try to wriggle out of it!"

"God forgive you! I'm only trying to be a bit cautious!"

"And if I bring you something that requires you to hurry up?"

Hajj Hussein was aware of the trap he was heading towards. His brother had not come to reprove him but as a suitor. But on whose behalf? All his children were married. Did he want her as a second wife for one of them? He resorted to silence, so as not to anger his brother, but the man did not give him a chance.

"What do you say?"

"Please God, it will turn out well!"

❧

Her mother kissed her and held her firmly.

She smelled her smell, as if she were still a baby. She washed her hair with oil and plaited it with fat. "The passionate Sukaina cools the fire inside me," she said, to tease her.

Sukaina smiled and was overcome by shyness.

"Daughter of true tribesmen. Daughter of true men, not a weak man among them!"

Sukaina was happy at the mention of her family. They were not village headmen but their number was unrivalled. On one embarrassing occasion the post of 'umda had almost come to them—the al-Badri family—from the al-Nayir family with their agreement. The 'umda Said al-Nayir had died and he didn't have a qualified successor. The eldest of his children, Muhammad, was in the capital studying at the Gordon Memorial College, in preparation for a future as a great efendi. Of his two sons, al-Bashir and al-Rashid, the elder was a youth of almost twenty but people thought him weak, and the younger was an embryo in his mother's belly. Hajar Narti discussed the affair and were at the point of transferring the headship to the al-Badri family, if it hadn't been for a telegram sent hastily to Muhammad Said al-Nayir, who arrived before his father had been buried to demand his inheritance. The al-Nayir family never forgot it, but love of the neighborhood concealed what was hidden in people's minds.

"Your father mentioned marriage," said her mother.

She smiled and shut her eyes.

"If it were up to me, I wouldn't have you married even to the Governor General, for who is equal to the fruit of my womb?"

Sukaina knew who was her equal but she didn't speak. She clung to her hopes and prayed.

"Your uncle has come with an acceptable bridegroom but your father will not make a decision without hearing your views."

Were her prayers being answered?

Her young heart fluttered in her breast. Had he really done as he had promised?

"A tribesman, a good man, with a good position."

What if the description fitted what she wanted and he got away?

He was a tribesman, a good young man, but what was a "good position?"

She looked at her mother nervously.

Let it be him. Let it be him. Let it be him. Let it be him. Let it be him. Then her mother spoke and everything she had been hoping for died.

※※

When Sukaina bint al-Badri was born, al-Bashir, the 'umda's son, was less than four years old.

He heard the ululations and leaped up with the boys to see what was going on. There were groups of children in short, dirty shirts. Playing barefoot in the water and sand had split their feet and made them rough. They jostled each other inquisitively among the women and went into the birthing house. The women chased them like chickens. But al-Bashir, head shaved against the lice, crept between feet until he reached the bed of the newly-born girl.

The room was redolent with the smell of smoke, mahaleb, and sandalwood to counter the smell of the birth water, but the young boy was not bothered by the smell. He looked at the wrinkled, purple-colored child, eyes closed, clutching her fists. "Do you like her, Bashir?" asked one of the women, as the boy laughed.

He craned his neck for a better look then said, "Sweet as a piece of wrapped chocolate!"

In the eyes of Bashir, Sukaina remained as sweet as a piece of wrapped chocolate, and his view didn't change as she grew up. When she went out to play with the boys and girls, he would give her a sugar stick stolen from the storeroom in their house, or an empty jar of Bint al-Sudan perfume with a picture of an African girl with bare breasts on it, wearing a red apron.

As she grew taller and joined the group of girls who collected firewood in the afternoon for the houses' kitchens, he would go out before them, collect what he could, put it on the road and hide. But Sukaina never ever carried it away. Her older companions appropriated it, thanking their lucky stars that they had stumbled on a bundle of ready firewood, leaving Sukaina and other girls her age to do their best to collect new wood.

Sukaina knew that the firewood was for her.

She knew who had left the firewood for her.

And Bashir knew that she knew, but he didn't say and she didn't reveal it.

The day she found firewood at the door of their house before she went out, she knew that was Bashir's promise to her. How could it not be, when he had left in the middle of the bundle of wood a full bottle of the Bint al-Sudan perfume?

The turtledove flew between them; the wind told each of them about the other, and both knew what their future would be.

If Babaker Sati hadn't come along.

※

An hour before dawn, Suleiman al-Hawati heard a voice calling.

He was sleepy. As he dozed off, his head flopped, then he woke in alarm. There was nothing except the waves whispering to each other and the hidden voices of the night, which gossiped about things humans are ignorant of. He didn't fear the corpse tied up a few feet away from him. Suleiman had seen a lot and was no longer afraid of dead bodies or their stories.

A few hours before, Fatima, the girl's mother, had come and seen the corpse, but had not found her daughter Su'ad. She went up and sat on a faraway mound, watching the darkness in silence. The years had taught Suleiman al-Hawati not to speak to her, for she did not reply. Instead, he filled a container with water, put it beside her, and withdrew to a distance to wait.

He amused himself by reciting a portion of the Qur'an, then chanted some praise of the Prophet, and sang some songs by 'Abd al-Rahman Ballas and al-Na'am Adam. His voice was hoarse and discordant but he amused himself. People have no companions like themselves and no entertainment like their own voices. Then sleep challenged him.

Whenever he dozed off, he would see the Nile flooding until it wetted his feet, at which point he would wake in alarm. When he realized he was dreaming, he would resume his silence again, and drowsiness would conquer him.

He continued his dialogue with sleep until he heard the call coming to him from the other bank. When he jumped up and looked, he saw the glow from the lamp carried by Hajj Bashir light up then go out, then light up again.

He shouted to let him know he was coming. Then he slipped into his boat and cut through the darkness, moving his oar through water he could not see. When he heard the sound of the oar planted in the heart of the waves, he pulled it, and heard a murmur flowing from the surface and returning to the depths.

He felt through the darkness towards a light that had been there and then was gone. He could see nothing, but he knew that the Nile was under him and his two friends were waiting for him. He could not have seen any less, had he really been blind. And he could not have been more certain of where he was headed, had he been able to see. Guided by his intuition and experience, he finally arrived.

He moored his boat on the other bank and was met by Hajj Bashir with his cough.

"What an hour, man!"

The two brothers walked down by the light of the lamp, holding the safety rope. They settled into the boat, then Suleiman pushed off and jumped in, barefoot, pants rolled up. As he rowed back, Hajj Bashir spat into the Nile.

"Your chest needs some treatment, Hajj!" said Rashid.

"How could I have the time? People's affairs leave no time for rest, man!"

Rashid knew that his brother made work for himself. He was always volunteering to take the lead and take things on, as if he was compensating for being deprived of his father's position thirty years ago.

The village—that had not considered the young Bashir suitable for the post of 'umda—could no longer do without him. He was almost the actual 'umda, while his brother—who was a year and a half, almost two years, older than him—lived like an efendi. Six months before, in December 1968, Muhammad Said had left behind all the business of the village and traveled to the capital to attend a concert by the Egyptian singer Umm Kulthum. It was said that he wore a European suit there and stayed up with his old colleagues from Gordon College. All of them had become efendis while he broke off his studies in his final year to become the 'umda of his village, then later became sheikh of the whole administrative district. As for Hajj Bashir, he never left his village or its people or its problems. If he traveled, it was to do something at court in Meroe or at the Agriculture Department in Al Goled. If there was a wedding in the village, it was he who supervised it, and if someone died, he was at the head of the gathering. If people needed a judgment on an inheritance, he was at the center of it—in spite of having failed to secure the inheritance of his late wife from the al-Badri family.

"Consult Ahmad Shigrib at least. You don't need to travel to the Dongola hospital."

"Are you mad, man? Is Shigrib good for anything except treating women and stomach pains? Shigrib only has one injection and sulfon-amide and Cafalgin pills."

He pronounced it like *kafi al-jinn.*

"You need butter and oil," said Suleiman.

Hajj Bashir smiled. "That's it. I'll make Nur al-Sham rub my chest with oil and I'll carry on drinking clarified butter."

As he finished his sentence, he was overcome by coughing. His body shook violently and he tried to hide his suffering with the sleeve of his cloak. He didn't see the stain it had caused, which was hidden by the darkness. Rashid hugged him tightly.

"By God, Hajj. I've tired myself for 'Abd al-Hafez's marriage more than he has."

"Kindness is never forgotten, my brother, kindness is never forgotten."

His voice became softer, as if he was about to mention her, but he quickly restrained himself. He said, "Then again, he's my wife's uncle and the grandfather of my son, so how could I not tire myself out for him?"

He didn't say her name but they heard it in the succession of his breaths. They couldn't see his face in the darkness but they knew there were tears in his eyes.

In a quivering voice, Suleiman al-Hawati said, "May God have mercy on her. She was an angel, by God. We never knew one like her, and never will!'

The three men were silent, overcome by the memory of the late beloved.

❦

Anyone who had not seen Sukaina bint al-Badri had not seen beauty.

❦

A warm breeze hit them, as the boat approached the jetty.

"Summer this year is like something from hell," said Hajj Bashir, as he tried to escape his memories.

No one replied. Suleiman jumped from his boat and pulled it to the shore, then stretched out his hand to help Hajj Bashir, who disembarked with difficulty, invoking the name of God, and coughing twice. Rashid jumped after him.

"Will you come back with us?" they asked Suleiman, as he stood in the muddy water.

"I'll guard the corpse until dawn. Then someone else will come."

"It will serve you well on Judgment Day, Suleiman!"

"May God not put an end to generosity, Hajj Bashir!"

He refused to take the cost of the journey from the two men, who left him and went up to where their mounts were tethered.

Rashid noticed Fatima, the mother of the young girl. Just an obscure black mass in the darkness, but he could identify her. She was sitting on the mound, watching the Nile and groaning for Su'ad.

"Hasn't the girl's mother lost hope after all these years?" he asked his brother, as he jumped onto his donkey,

"It's a mother's heart. Rashid. It's said her husband left her years ago and married again and had children. The poor woman asks for no one in her life but Su'ad!"

"But after all these years! What is the sense in what she is doing?"

"It's love, man!"

Rashid turned to his brother. He could see his face clearly this time. It was lit up with memories.

✿

They parted near their houses. Rashid headed south towards his empty house, where he lived alone without a wife and invited his companions to wine and games parties, while he went to his two brothers' houses to eat.

Hajj Bashir made his way in the darkness, relying on his donkey's knowledge of the way, until he reached his pen.

He got down from the donkey and was about to tie him up when he heard a call from inside the house. "Hajj?"

He shouted a reply and the door opened. Nur al-Sham, his wife, came out carrying a lamp to dispel the darkness. Behind her was one of the Arab girls that helped her.

Nur al-Sham was of medium height, slim, in her mid-thirties. She wore her hair in thin plaits, and had nothing of her aunt in her except for her eyes.

"I've waited up for you."

He was tender, as always. There were few men like him in Hajar Narti, or indeed, in the whole of the district.

Perhaps it was love that had softened his heart of old and had made him gentle with women.

It annoyed him that his wife should stay up till dawn waiting for him to return. He was about to excuse himself, but she forestalled him.

"You must go to Sheikh Muhammad's. He sent asking for you more than once."

"What has happened?"

"I don't know. But his messages have never stopped! He insisted that you go to him when you returned."

"It's dawn!"

"His last message insisted that you respond to him, even if it is at the Hour of Resurrection!"

"O Lord, O Protector!"

39

Hajj Bashir left his donkey without tying it up. He lifted his robe and hurried away. "The lamp, Hajj!" Nur al-Sham called after him.

But he didn't stop, not even to light the lamp he was carrying. He was running and coughing, chest almost splitting, but he didn't stop. He went down a hill of sand and turned off to the left between the houses. He wasn't thinking. His heart could not bear to think about what might have happened. Let it be anything, except for harm to have come to his brother.

Eleven years ago, he had run along the same route, but in the opposite direction. He was running from the house of his brother Muhammad Said to his house to catch her. Today, he was chasing a fever and bad news. But he was late. He was late for the second time. And unlike the first time, this time did not have another to follow.

Now he was running to the house of his brother. Inside, there was a repeated shout, "Don't do it, Muhammad. Don't do it, my brother!"

He was afraid—afraid of losing someone he loved. He had no thought except that something bad had happened. So, as he was about to enter Muhammad Said's house, which was bathed in darkness, he was startled when he heard his brother's voice calling him. Coughing hard, he stopped and leaned on the wall of the house. As he coughed and spat, he felt his body collapsing, but his brother caught him, held him up, and helped him reach where he had been sitting under the acacia tree in front of the house.

Hajj Bashir lay on the wooden bed, panting. He spat several times. As he felt his mouth fill with stale food, he wiped it with the hem of his gown.

Muhammad Said handed him something to drink, put his hand on his head, and comforted him.

"You're okay, my brother, you'll be okay!"

Some time passed and Hajj Bashir settled. His cough grew calmer, though his chest was still splitting with every breath.

"Bashir, you must see a doctor!"

He waved his hand in objection, although he could not speak. His brother did not waste the opportunity. "How long have you been coughing like this? Your body has become so thin that we can hardly tell who you are!"

Hajj Bashir shook his head.

"You are stubborn. You use work as an excuse. Look after your health, Bashir. Don't be childish!"

"You never let go of your faith in hospital medicine, as if you were still a student at Gordon College," said Hajj Bashir, who had found his voice at last, to reprove his brother.

"And you still hate hospitals as though this wasn't 1969. We're not in the 1940s, brother. We have medicine and doctors and science now!"

"My cure lies in butter and oil, don't worry!"

"You are as stubborn as your grandmother, al-Afiya."

"And you summoned me at dawn and killed me with worry. What's going on?"

Muhammad Said glowered. Hajj Bashir couldn't see his face in the darkness, but he realized it when his voice came out.

"Telegrams have arrived from Khartoum. Orders from the military."

Hajj Bashir was shocked. What did they have to do with the military?

"What do they want?"

"Telegrams of support."

"They took power by force, and they are asking for support?"

"Some people did not wait for them to demand it. The radio has been broadcasting telegrams of support since sunset. Cities, villages, prominent men, and societies. Have you heard of the village of Salilayha in Gezira?"

He said he hadn't.

"Salilayha sent four telegrams of allegiance, which have been broadcast more than once."

"What's that got to do with us, Muhammad? We're Khatmiyya, and our allegiance is to the Mirghanis and the Unionist Party!"

"We're 'umdas, Bashir, before we're Khatmiyya."

"And our allegiance?"

"What's the value of loyalty, if we lose power?"

Hajj Bashir stretched out his hand in the darkness and groped until he found the small pail. He filled a glass and drank it in one gulp.

"And why should we lose it?" he asked in protest. "We have been the 'umdas in Hajar Narti since the time of the Turks. The al-Nayir family is older than any authority in Khartoum!"

"They're the military, Bashir!"

"They're the military in Khartoum. And we're the al-Nayir family in Hajar Narti. We were sheikhs and 'umdas and governors before the British, before al-Azhari, before 'Abboud with his military and the revolution with its parties."

"They detained 'Abboud, Bashir, they detained all the party leaders!"

Hajj Bashir's heart raced. Al-Azhari himself? The leader of the country? The liberator, who raised the flag of independence? Sidi al-Azhari Ismail, who wears a suit of coarse fabric? The military detained him after the 1958 coup, then fell and al-Azhari remained. Would they not learn? He had called his son al-Azhari after the liberator, so why, whenever the military came, did they jail the liberator? Why did they point their guns at the leader instead of at the enemy? He had been opposed to the military in his heart since the time of Babaker Sati. But Babaker fought the Italians. He didn't fight al-Azhari!

"Don't you think it's like their previous coup?"

"No, Bashir. This time, they are said to be communists!"

"Communists?"

"They have Babaker 'Awad Allah with them, the judge. They've appointed him as Prime Minister."

"Who's he?"

"He's from El Geteina. He was with me at Gordon College but he studied law."

"Has the whole world gone mad?"

"Even Egypt welcomed the coup."

"'Abd al-Nasser? He was here recently! He made peace with King Faisal here in al-Mahjoub's house!"

Muhammad Said muttered, "And Umm Kulthum was here. And I've certainly never heard al-Mahjoub's name among the detainees. But every name in your head is in jail now. Don't talk to me about us being in charge. If we don't pledge our allegiance to the new authority quickly, power could pass from us to your in-laws."

Muhammad Said knew his brother's weak point. He was always needing to assert his neutrality to the al-Badri family. In every situation in which the al-Nayir family was opposed to the al-Badri family, the eyes of everyone, including relatives, were directed to Hajj Bashir, expecting him to be neutral. And in every situation in which the al-Nayir family was opposed to the al-Badri family, Hajj Bashir was forced into an extreme position against his in-laws so as not to be accused of siding with them.

"I am your charge sheet in your family's eyes," as Sukaina used to say to him.

And after her, his charge sheet was Nur al-Sham.

"What do you think, Bashir?"

"I wouldn't go against you, brother!"

Muhammad Said sighed contentedly.

"It is in God's hands. We'll send telegrams of allegiance right away. One from me, as sheikh of the Hajar Narti district, and the villages belonging to it. One from you, as representative of the citizens of Hajar Narti. And one from Nur al-Sham, your wife, as representative of the Women's Union."

"Will that be enough to spare us the evil of the military?"

"Nothing will be enough to spare us the evil of the military, Bashir. Nothing is enough to spare us. But it's all we can do."

FAYIT NIDDU WAS BORN around 1924.

There is no official document to confirm this. The recollections of her relatives are muddled and do not confirm anything. But all their suspicions revolve around the year that witnessed a rebellion of the Sudanese army, followed by the departure of the Egyptian army from the country.

Momentous events happened in the capital but the rebellions lost most of their precision and order by the time they reached Hajar Narti, despite the involvement of the local population in them. Some people say she was born after it happened, while others say she was a baby when news of the rebellion reached them. A lot of people were confused about the time, when groups from the al-Badri family signed a note which was delivered in Khartoum demanding British protection for the country, and the al-Nayir family supported demonstrations chanting "Long live Egypt," in which some of their young people who were studying at Gordon College took part. That year was full of events, all important, but some more important than others, so people forgot when 'Izz al-Qawm, the 'umda Said al-Nayir's servant, delivered her daughter Fayit Niddu.

Fayit Niddu was born in a room of fresh mudbrick, which is still to be found in the house of the old 'umda. When the 1946 flood came to Hajar Narti, the 'umda's house disappeared in the angry waters of the Nile, except for part of the guest room and 'Izz al-Qawm's room.

That room had seen men enter it in the dead of night. It had witnessed late-night conversations, groans, unanswered pleas, the snorting of men as their tensions were released, and several births, followed by the death of the children. Of more than twenty births, only three survived, of whom the youngest was Fayit Niddu.

'Izz al-Qawm was brought as a child with her mother from the extreme south of the country. She was bought by al-Afiya, the legendary grandmother of the al-Badri family, who gave the two of them to her son al-Nayir on the occasion of his marriage.

'Izz al-Qawm grew up knowing nowhere except Hajar Narti. She spoke Arabic with a northern accent, while her mother, who had been brought from the south, continued learning Arabic with a foreign accent until she died at the age of nearly a hundred. Senile at the time of her death, she was al-Afiya's last friend, and the person who spoke most about her. Her stories about her were a mixture of love and hatred, of senility and tortuous language.

As for 'Izz al-Qawm, she lived through the official abolition of slavery—the British laws that broke the back of local society. She carried on praying to God in the hearing of her masters. "May the British be blessed by the masters and sheikhs, and may the Arabs have less and never find more!"

Her masters heard her prayers and laughed. No one dared to scold her except for Hajja Radiya at the end of her life, but the old slave didn't care about the anger of this daughter of aristocrats. The men pleaded her case, so Hajja Radiya kept quiet about her, though she was even more angry inside.

The first time Fayit Niddu tried men was with 'Abd al-Razeq.

She was a young girl and he was a young boy.

He came into the room of her mother 'Izz al-Qawm, drunk. A young boy with one foot in the world of men and one foot in children's games. He had been drinking the local wine with his companions until he thought himself the King of Britain. Then the devils fought over his passions and his hunger for women stirred. The wine led him on to try the 'umda's servant, so his reputation in bed would rival that of his elders. The young boy came in, asking for 'Izz al-Qawm, who was almost sixty.

She had spent all her life as a slave in the 'umda's house, serving in the kitchen, making arak, and satisfying men.

She had borne twenty children or more, from a thousand men or more. She didn't know who the fathers were. She wasn't counting and she didn't care. She obeyed, she prayed for the British, she prayed against the Arabs, and her children died —some with names and some without names. Only Wazin al-Dahab, known as Dahab for short, 'Abd al-Tamm, and Niddu escaped death.

They escaped death but they did not escape life.

Dahab married a slave of a notable in the town of Al Dabbah. 'Abd al-Tamm fled to Khartoum in disgrace and secured a government manumission document, through which he got a job in the Gezira agricultural project in Central Sudan, or so it was said. His mother, 'Izz al-Qawm, couldn't understand why her son had left a job on the 'umda's project to work on the British project so far away from her! Agriculture was agriculture and the British were good people but so were the al-Nayir family. So why did he choose to be so far away from her? She never forgave him for deserting her until the day she died.

As for Fayit Niddu, the youngest child and the last to escape, she stayed under the feet of her mother, playing, serving, and learning allegiance to the 'umda's family, and obedience to men. It was just that the 'umda Said al-Nayir was no longer called her master but her uncle.

'Abd al-Razeq, blind drunk, came upon them in her mother's room in her uncle's house. He surprised her mother, and the old woman gently reproached him, but he pulled her hard and gripped her hand firmly to set it on his penis.

'Izz al-Qawm cried out, imploring him to stop.

"My child, say *bismillah*!"

But he was drunk to the eyeballs. He lifted his shirt, pulled out his member, and said in a heavy voice, "*Bismillah*."

The old woman laughed, grabbed his member and stroked it gently. "My boy!" she said. "If the 'umda Said caught you, he would cut it off and your aged aunt would no longer be of use for anything."

He threw himself on her until they both fell on the ground. He couldn't hear a word of what she said. Fayit Niddu was absorbed in herself, almost sinking into the earth she was lying on. She shut her eyes, so as not to see the boy—who was almost the same age as her—trying to penetrate her mother, and the old woman gently maneuvered to avoid it.

He was confused by the novelty of the experience, and his drunkenness played with him so he woke up while his penis slept, and felt dizzy when it was erect. The old woman didn't help him onto herself so he found himself at a loss, not knowing where to penetrate. He cursed and spat, stood up dizzily and turned his back on the old woman. Then he lost his balance and fell down beside Fayit Niddu, who was digging in the ground to escape. She was crying silently, crying without tears, while beside her 'Abd al-Razeq had fallen on his back.

Did he maneuver toward her intentionally or did he, in his drunken state, imagine she was the old woman he was wrestling with? He stretched out his hand and touched Fayit Niddu's leg. He felt her taut, youthful skin, and passed his hand over it. The young girl trembled, curled up, and clenched her fists in fear.

'Izz al-Qawm called out in desperation, "'Abd al-Razeq! Seek guidance from God, do not create a scandal for us!"

Perhaps the boy imagined that the voice came from the body he was passing his fingers over. He mumbled something abruptly, then thrust his body on top of the girl, and flattened her. She could not find the strength to push him off her. His hand fumbled with her clothes until he had stripped her naked. He belched up wine then sent his penis on its way. And in the soft, youthful body it did not go astray; it knew its way and penetrated her. Fayit Niddu shouted as if she was being split in two.

In the last corner of darkness, 'Izz al-Qawm whispered noiselessly, "May the Arabs have less and never find more! May the Arabs have less and never find more!"

Fayit Niddu beat the dawn every day.

Dawn never caught her sleeping. She would stir in the darkness immediately before dawn; prepare her utensils; steam her glasses; mix the cardamom, ginger, and cloves; boil the coffee beans, then pound them in a wooden mortar until they became soft.

Abir would wake to the beating of the mortar. She would get up like a dirty autumn river, brow wrinkled, and eyes swollen, surrounded by sticky pus. Then, leaning her back against the wall, she would scratch her hair.

Fayit Niddu called her reproachfully, "Abir, you sleep as if you had not a care in the world!"

No answer.

Her mother ran between the various things she needed in the morning.

"Today is the first night of 'Abd al-Hafez's henna party!"

'Abd al-Hafez was her father, or so she had heard in the secret gossip of the village. Her birth certificate was written in the name of Muhammad Said, for she had been born in his house to a slave of his family, but who in the village did not know that she was the daughter of 'Abd al-Hafez ibn al-Hussein al-Badri? Her aunt was Sukaina bint al-Badri, the most beautiful woman to tread the soil in Hajar Narti.

"You will go to the wedding venue before the *iftar*, to serve them and attend to their needs," said her mother.

Abir nodded her head.

"Your aunt Dahab may come today, or perhaps tomorrow. If she arrives before I am there, send a message to me in the shack."

Abir received the instructions in silence. She would carry them out but she was not obliged to speak.

Hajja al-Radiya hated this silence of hers more than anyone. She nicknamed her "The Owl," though the men and boys found her attractive. She was thin and silent as a dumb goat, but she was attractive and as generous as a tribe of harlots, refusing no one, so the young men called her "The Bitch."

As for her mother, she teased her by calling her "The Doctor," when she was relaxed. The dream that Hajja Radiya resisted, but it was still alive and breathing.

Fayit Niddu went out into the courtyard of the house, looking for the jars of arak. She had closed them five days ago and was sure she had secured the lids. The Jaw dates were fermenting inside the containers and the night would begin with boiling and straining them. There would be European alcohol—"Christian raki," as Fayit Niddu called it, in imitation of her mother—like gin or sherry or beer. But Fayit Niddu's arak had no competitor. She was highly skilled, and she only made it for very special occasions.

People would remember 'Abd al-Hafez wad al-Badri's wedding for a long time, and they would remember for all time how they got drunk on Fayit Niddu's arak.

❦

Fayit Niddu left her little house at sunrise.

It was a narrow courtyard with a single room in it, and two leaning walls with no door. Resting on the room was a roof of palm leaves propped up with sticks of firewood. The rear wall of the house had one side of it collapsing under the weight of a hill of sand. This was the exit that was used to go out into the open air to defecate. Urination was done in any corner of the courtyard, after which water would be sprinkled over it.

Fayit Niddu left this wreck of a place that she called home and as the sun rose walked the long path to the west toward the port. Her body had prominent muscles, like those of a man at the height of his virility. But her forty-year-old expression retained a remarkable feminine beauty.

Her foot sunk in the sand and she vigorously extracted it. With her right hand she held a bundle on her head, while her left hand hung down, carrying a cloth bag. She passed between the houses of the village, which were shaking off their sleep. She was met by Hajj Bashir on his donkey, on his way to send telegrams of allegiance for the new regime in the capital. He was beset by worries, so did not see the woman passing by. She shouted to him in greeting but he did not reply. "People are so busy!" she said to herself.

As the houses stopped, the sand stopped, and under Fayit Niddu's feet the ground turned to black, fertile soil. She made her way along narrow paths between the palm trees, and at one of the gardens of the Badri family she heard the sound of ghajar.

She could see a group of them—men, women, and children—all together, camped under the palm tree. Some of them were asleep, and some of them were turning over pots, or looking for things in pails full of rubbish. Some women were looking around the place, picking up dates that had dropped from the palm trees. They were still green, and as big as a lotus fruit, but they ate them with pleasure. The children wandered half naked, their bottom halves uncovered.

Fayit Niddu stood by them and shouted in a loud voice, "Curse you! You're vermin, just like rats!"

Some of them responded by pretending not to hear, while others gave a hoarse laugh.

"Don't you have a country of your own? May God cut you off!"

"The land is God's land and we're God's servants," replied a woman in a thick, expressionless voice.

Ghajari voices, both men's and women's, were always neutral in tone, and the person hearing them couldn't tell whether they were joking or angry. They were like an instrument with just one string.

They didn't care if they were cursed, and they never got tired of being rejected. They came in groups and left in groups. They sought sustenance in wandering and they fed themselves by scavenging.

They had no connections with any place or person, except for a single story about al-Afiya and Bahiya, which 'Izz al-Qawm told, having heard it from her senile mother. No one else told it and no one knew whether it was true or false, but it explained some of what Hajar Narti had seen but not understood.

Apart from that, people regarded them as rats, as Fayit Niddu called them. They regarded them as rubbish and their arrival as a disease.

Fayit Niddu spat between her feet.

"You don't know God! May God spare us your heresy!"

A naked child urinated near her as if in reply, and she went on her way, keeping her anger to herself. She hated to see her village being ravaged by ghajar every year. Before she became hidden by the palm trees, a stone came her way, without hitting her, and she heard a thick, expressionless voice curse her, "Servant!"

She turned around and saw the group silently staring at her. "Praise be to God," she shouted at them. "Servant! My master is an 'umda, better than ghajar who smell of copper."

No one took any notice of her. No one cared. She hurried on her way, raising the black earth, as she called on God to give the earth rest from the ghajari rats.

❧

The story of al-Afiya and the ghajari Bahiya belonged to no particular time and its details were imprecise. Like all popular stories, it changed every time it was told. Something was added here and something subtracted there. The name of one place was replaced by another one; a new, resounding expression was introduced. But it always retained its principal structure, with its two basic characters, al-Afiya, the ancestor of the al-Nayir family, and the ghajari Bahiya.

Muhammad al-Hasan, the ancestor of the al-Nayir family, married al-Afiya, who was a stranger to Hajar Narti. Al-Afiya would tell stories about herself in the first years, saying she was the daughter of a great Shayqiyya warrior. 'Izz al-Din's mother, the only person to relate it, spoke of bloody battles that al-Afiya's father had taken part in and remembered the poetry that had been recited to lament him when he died. But the poetry disappeared when al-Afiya passed and 'Izz al-Qawm forgot what her mother had composed.

Years later, al-Afiya would declare that she was a descendant of the sheikhs of the Warariq near Sab al-Zubairiya. She would spread around this story after the great storms that swept Sab al-Zubairyya away, so no one would know the truth.

After some years in Hajar Narti, and with the rise of the al-Nayir family, al-Afiya would change her story and connect herself with Hajar Narti, saying that her grandfather was one of the founders of the village. She would angrily confront anyone who said that she belonged somewhere other than the village that was governed by her family.

All the many stories agreed on one thing: al-Afiya's young age when she married Muhammad al-Hasan. She was a slim, sickly girl of no more than sixteen, but she was strong-minded and determined. Her tough personality had been born with her and accompanied her to the husband she had never known before her marriage.

'Izz al-Qawm told—on the authority of her mother—of the surprise that confronted the young bride.

On her first night with her husband, the other women prepared her with a massage, sandalwood, and incense. She was naked, her body wrapped in a bridal gown, which was unfastened and needed only a touch for it to fall and reveal everything. But the bridegroom showed no interest in his bride.

He embraced her a little and played on her body with his hands. Then he sighed and turned his back on her.

Al-Afiya was afraid.

The sounds of ululations resounded outside. The noise of the partygoers had not yet died down but the bridegroom turned his back on her and tried to sleep.

Like any well brought up girl, she accepted his behavior with humility. She fastened her bridal dress, lay down beside him, and carried on listening to his irregular breathing until morning.

She didn't betray him when the women met her the following day. She met all the questions, looks, and a few touches from the old women with a show of shyness.

One old woman said to her, "Tell us, girl! Tell your aunts the good news of your wedding night!"

But al-Afiya ignored them. As night drew near, she eagerly used more massage oil and sandalwood, and smeared her body with a lot of fat and oil.

Muhammad Hasan came in, greeted her, and stood looking at her for a long time. Al-Afiya thought of taking off her dress but her upbringing stopped her. It wasn't right for girls from good families to respond too quickly or make any seductive moves. Otherwise, what would there be to distinguish them from slave girls?

A servant could reveal her desires, and indeed always had to exhibit feelings of pleasure even if she faked them, but girls of good families didn't do that.

Muhammad al-Hasan put out the light. Al-Afiya thought it was embarrassment that had got in his way last night, but tonight he would take advantage of the darkness. She changed position to make it easier for him to reach her in the darkness of the room.

He put his hand on her.

Now what had to happen would happen.

She heard him breathing beside her face. He put a cold kiss on her cheek, embraced her, and stretched her out on the wooden bed. He moved over her, touched her breasts with his hands, and felt the side of her thigh. His breathing was erratic like the previous day, but after that, nothing. He put a kiss on the bridge of her nose, then gave up. Two bodies in a dark room on a narrow bed, surrounded by tension and the smells of local perfumes.

Al-Afiya didn't deliberately do it but she moved her leg and her thigh touched her husband. Nothing.

Nothing she had heard from the older women in the weeks preceding her marriage about men's tent-pegs, or the member like the leg of a wooden bed, was there. It was just a quick touch, but all she felt was a piece of cold flesh. She fidgeted again and her suspicions were confirmed. Nothing.

No tent-peg, no column, no bed leg. Just a piece of flesh like those she could see on children.

Nothing in her had aroused her husband.

The pair spent a second night without sleep.

When did al-Afiya realize what would arouse her husband?

Sometimes, 'Izz al-Qawm's mother said it happened on the second night, sometimes she said that it happened weeks later, and once she said months later.

One could not trust the stories she told in her old age, especially when she told them out of revenge. But all her stories, despite their differences, agreed that al-Afiya lost her virginity the night her husband plucked up his courage and penetrated her carrying a whip.

Was it on the third night, as she waited in her bridal gown, or was it after she had stopped waiting?

We will never know that, but we do know that al-Afiya never forgot the night Muhammad al-Hasan revealed his secret, so long as she lived.

It was the night that led her to Bahiya the ghajari.

✦

Abir did not stay long after her mother had left.

She washed her face with a little water and smoothed her dirty, untidy hair. She looked for her sandals but could not find them. She tried to remember, had she brought them back yesterday? She didn't bother to think too hard, but went out barefoot, heading to the wedding venue. What importance were sandals for a young servant on a day like this? Even if she put them on, she would take them off at the wedding venue and serve barefoot, and in the end they would be lost there.

She slipped along the village paths, passing groups of farmers on their way to work. She noticed some women walking in front of her toward Hussein al-Badri's house—women who were politely offering to help for fear of being criticized.

She walked behind them. As she passed near Muhammad Said's house, she saw the enormous man, who radiated gravity and authority, sitting under the acacia tree listening intently to the radio. As she approached the surgery, she saw Ahmad Shigrib standing in front of it cleaning his teeth, an iron bowl in his hand. When Shigrib noticed Abir, he spat out what was in his mouth.

He smiled at her, and she answered him with a cold look.

He turned around, looked, and satisfied himself that the women could not see him. The path was empty. He waved to her.

Would he make her late for the wedding venue?

Perhaps he would, but she responded to his wave. He made way for her and she went into the surgery. After he had put down the bowl and followed her in, he shut the iron door and made a noise as if to tell people where they were. Shigrib was aroused, but Abir did not care.

She stood looking at him. He moved closer to her and pointed to his bed, laid on the ground.

Ahmad Shigrib lived in the surgery room and had his food brought from Muhammad's Said's house every mealtime. His clothes and other necessities were in two large cardboard boxes, and beside them were dozens of books, piled up in a tall stack, with a new radio on top of them.

On the wall of the room were two medical posters, one of them showing the anatomy of the human body and the circulatory system, and the second giving instructions for vaccinating against childhood diseases, beside a picture of a woman giving her breasts to her baby to suckle. On the wall beside them was a phrase in slanted handwriting which Ahmad Shigrib had written during his first days at the surgery: "Long live the struggle of the working class… long live the struggle of the people!"

Abir sat on the bed.

Shigrib's eyes lit up. "I've wanted you since yesterday," he told her.

She looked into his eyes coldly.

He wished she weren't so quiet, but she aroused him nonetheless. He threw himself down beside her then stretched out his hand to caress her cheek. Her eyes did not blink, as she gazed silently into his eyes.

He lowered his hand to her neck, then to her girlish chest, which he pinched, as the young girl shuddered. Taking a deep breath, he then pulled her to his chest and whispered to her in a feverish voice, "I want you!"

He threw himself on her girlish lips with all the impetuosity of his desire.

'Abd al-Razeq was hanging around at the edge of the Agricultural Project channel.

His work was important but undemanding. He was the channel's watchman. He began his day at the water pump, where he would take off his cloak and stand in his short shirt. He would crank the machine to start it; it would creak and smoke would rise. Then the thumps would assume a rhythm and the water would pour out.

'Abd al-Razeq's job after that was to follow the muddy channel to check how the water was flowing. He would check that the channel wasn't overflowing anywhere and make sure none of the farmers were stealing a share of the irrigation water on a day they weren't supposed to. He would walk up and down the channel like a soldier on patrol, singing as he walked.

He had a good voice and a good heart. He also had two wives. One was his cousin and the second was Hasna, from the nearby village of Al-Konj. These two wives competed with each other to serve him. He would go to his work in the morning, content as a well-watered palm tree.

He walked to the north towards Fayit Niddu's shack, where the farmers had gathered, as well as people waiting for the ferry to cross to the other bank, and people looking for gossip. A lot of people would come after the discovery of the drowned body. And 'Abd al-Razeq would spend several hours chatting and drinking coffee.

As he approached the shack he heard Hussein al-Badri's distinctive laugh. A shriek-laugh like no other, from a heart like the heart of a child. Time had not broken him, nor had disasters shaken him. A man in his eighties, who had been tried by the loss of more than one son and a daughter, and blessed with a troop of grandchildren. People talked of how handsome he was in his youth—fair skinned, with a bulky frame, and scars thin as a shadow. He loved drinking sessions and talking to the slave girls. The year when a group of notables from Hajar Narti made the pilgrimage, with the 'umda Said al-Nayir at their head, Hussein al-Badri came back from the Port of Jeddah with boxes of sherry. That year was called the "Pilgrimage Year" because more than thirty men and women made the pilgrimage together from the village. The day they returned, sheep and calves were slaughtered, and cups of broth were laid out in the streets of Hajar Narti. The eulogist and dervishes came, and the Qur'an was read more than once. The eulogists sang until their pockets were full of money; then, at midnight, Hussein al-Badri's boxes were opened, and pilgrims, guests, and some of the dervishes got drunk. The more mischievous of the youths also had a share.

'Abd al-Razeq came into the shack but did not find any space. Hussein al-Badri was sitting and people were crowding to hear his stories and enjoy his playful responses.

When he arrived, the old man was finishing a story called something like "The man who hasn't got anything big buys something big." 'Abd al-Razeq didn't hear him telling it but—like everyone sitting there—he knew the story. And like everyone sitting there he laughed in appreciation as if nothing had escaped him.

Hussein al-Badri didn't leave his audience time for their attention to wane. With no preliminaries, he moved on to another story.

"Of course, you all know the story of the old man of the Mukabarab."

The audience responded with smiles and laughter. "Tell it!" or "Tell it, for God's sake!" various voices said to him.

He leaned his cheek against his stick and looked around at those present. "They say that a merchant took his goods around the land of the Mukabarab."

"The Mukabarab in the land of the Ja'alin," someone muttered, as if to finish the sentence.

Hussein al-Badri paid him no attention.

"A group of Mukabarab children attacked the man and robbed him. Then they told him that he wouldn't go until they banged the *dallouka* for him and he danced." Some of the audience laughed. "The man implored them not to deprive him of his honor after robbing him of his goods but they insisted. The children banged the *dallouka* and the man danced, then they let him go. The poor man walked on a little until he met one of the Mukabarab notables, who was very grave and serious. He hurried to him to complain. 'Uncle! Help me! I'm in a wretched state!' When he asked him what was the matter, and the merchant told him what had happened to him, the old man replied with regret, 'The wretched one is your uncle, who wasn't there when you danced!'"

The audience laughed until the Nile waves surged.

The same stories as usual. People fed them to each other, for they loved gossip.

'Abd al-Razeq noticed some strange faces among the crowd. He bent down to whisper to the nearest member of the audience, "The group from Sarwa?"

"Yes, but the corpse isn't one of theirs."

"A corpse of the jinn, then, this one! What disaster sent it in our direction?"

"Probably, they'll bury it today."

"Suleiman said it might be another day."

"So you believe Suleiman's lies? Suleiman says anything he likes."

Husein al-Badri's voice rang out as he stood up, and the pair's whispering was brought to an end. In his booming voice, he said, "Today, people, is the henna ceremony of my son, 'Abd al-Hafez. Anyone who does not honor us by attending, we will cut him off till the day of judgment."

Congratulations echoed all around the shack.

Hussein al-Badri repeated his message to stress his point. Then he laid into the shack door as he went out, and the place breathed a sigh of relief. Some farmers who worked with him followed him to ask his opinion or go over a problem.

As he spoke to them, he noticed her in the same place she never left.

Fatima, the girl's mother, sitting, waiting for the River Nile to spew out more of its victims. She was being eaten by the sun, but she had not looked for shade.

Hussein al-Badri looked at her and remembered the fruit of his heart that had been crushed.

Why did the pain not eat me away as it did you, Fatima?

Was Su'ad more precious than Sukaina?

The mother of the young girl always reminded him of what he had done.

If only you could forget, Fatima. If only you could come back to the wide world with its beauty that you renounced.

But he knew that Fatima was not about to forget Su'ad.

❧

They say that if the River Nile spews out a drowned man, it follows it with another two victims it had taken before.

Fatima came and waited. Sometimes the River Nile confirms what is said and spews out the corpses of old victims, forgotten by their families and the waves in its depths. Fatima examined what the Nile had given up but did not find Su'ad.

❧

Su'ad was ten years old when she went out.

She was like no other child.

Su'ad was born with a small, flat head and a prominent brow. Her eyes were split, with heavy brows. She laughed as if she were talking to the angels.

She didn't learn to speak quickly.

The relatives said sadly, "She's blessed."

The efendis said wisely, "A Mongol."

And Fatima said insistently, "She's my daughter."

Su'ad lived for ten years in the bosom of her family.

Fatima kept the world from her as birds do from their young.

Then she went out, barefoot, in a village who all knew her. She walked on, distributing smiles to the sun, to walls, sand, donkeys, palm trees, mango trees, and orange groves.

Then the Nile took her.

❧

"'ABD AL-HAFEZ, CONGRATULATIONS! Today is your day, bridegroom!"

"Congratulations!" the girls repeated.

Wazin al-Dahab's voice cut through the evening in Hussein al-Badri's house. She beat her drum with enthusiasm and sang as loud as she could.

Around her was a group of girls and young women.

The decorations were a festival of colors. Every girl had made an effort to shine on a day when the young people came together. Suddenly one of them got up to dance. She moved her bare feet over the ground, stirring up the dust, and as she bent her top half backwards, her breasts and bottom stood out. Then she spread her arms like the wings of a dove about to fly, shutting her eyes and making her neck dance left and right. She danced as if she was soaring far away. She was no longer a female, she was free, and the plaits of her hair were spread over her neck—or even her back if they were lucky.

After a little dancing, one of the boys leaped towards her, spurred on by the vigor of manhood and supported by the singing and shouts of his companions. He shook his hand over her and slammed his foot hard on the ground. The girl greeted him by leaning her head toward him, touching his chest with her flying locks.

The bold, lucky youth went back to his companions who received him with laughter, and the girl continued to dance as if embracing the clouds.

The bridegroom, 'Abd al-Hafez, sat on a short wooden bed in the midst of a crowd of old women who put liniment on his feet and henna on his massive legs and giant palms.

There were lamps and incandescent mantles in every corner of the vast courtyard. The guests sat in circles in scattered groups. Every group had its own preoccupations.

Hajj Bashir moved between them all, to make certain that everything was in order. "Hurry up, you lot!" he shouted to the servants.

Every time he shouted, he coughed.

He didn't stop shouting and didn't stop coughing. In the morning he had seen blood on his jilbab. But he was determined not to say anything.

The village was busy with the guests so there was no time for complaining. He struggled against the illness that was flowing from his chest, tiring him out, and spreading everywhere. He came across the father of the bride, Hajj Hussein al-Badri, and they smiled at one another and walked away.

The two men were joined by an old affection—an affection that was stronger than any competition between the two houses of al-Nayir and al-Badri. Hajj Bashir did not care about any sectarian dispute, even though the former belonged to the Khatmiyya order while the others owed allegiance to the Mahdi's supporters.

The slaughtered animals hung outside the house. The young men carried the animal meat at a run to the group of women in the kitchen who were supervised by Hajja al-Radiya. Fayit Niddu and her fellow former slaves grilled the meat, soaked it in gravy, and turned the rice over.

Hajja Radiya shouted, "These girls today are useless! Is this service? Is this cooking? They've abandoned women's work and given themselves over to stupidity and rudeness!"

She was starting to turn over the grilled meat when several women hurried toward her. "Leave it, Radiya, we'll take care of that!"

As she reluctantly handed it over to them, the old woman who was always angry turned to the young men carrying the meat. "What are you waiting for? You're just prancing beside the women. Put down what you're carrying and get out and go back to the men's place, if you are men yourselves!"

They fled from her. Hajja Radiya was as frightening as fires in the palms. And the older she got, the more bad tempered she became. She always said she hated "rudeness" and "bastards."

Beside the dead animals a group of youths were hovering around a tambour player, who was singing.

I'm not your match, Buthayna,
I'm not a good omen for what you deserve
If your happiness is in money,
Then my situation needs no explanation.

The young men sighed in sorrow for a love killed by poverty. Everyone sighed as he imagined Buthayna. They could dream, but there was no Buthayna there. It was just wishful thinking.

Rashid hurried past them. Someone called to him and he waved his hand in greeting, then went on. A Nile crocodile was chasing its prey. Amid that crowd of preoccupied people, Rashid had decided to catch the prey that had been occupying his attention.

He went past the kitchen and saw the women crowded around the food. Hajja Radiya was giving out orders and the women were running quickly to obey.

He went out to the dance floor. Dahab was lighting up the night.

The girls stirred up the earth dancing, and the boys were about to fly from happiness. All these beautiful bodies in colorful clothes dancing for them. The time for wine had not arrived yet. If they found it now, the world would explode.

Girls dancing, Dahab's sweet voice, and wine. Could a young man wish for more than that?

Rashid looked for Abir but could not find her. He decided to follow her tracks; he searched in the out-of-the-way places where the light dies and darkness dwells, and he found some men in a hurry with other girls. The men greeted him with nervous laughs and the girls tried to hide their faces out of modesty, but he had no interest in anyone else.

Where was Ahmad Shigrib?

He passed by the groups a second time, looking for him. Perhaps if he found him, he would find Abir hiding in his eyes.

He went into the men's diwan, where leading figures from the whole district were sitting separately. In front of them was the best grilled meat and broth chosen by the women, as well as bottles of beer and sherry that had not yet been touched. They were engrossed in politics when Rashid came in, and his brother, Muhammad Said, was talking.

"In Khartoum, be afraid of just three things: God, electricity, and the military. Here we are safe for a while. We fear God, the flood, and worms in the dates."

Someone from the al-Badri family replied to him, "The President of the Revolutionary Command Council is a Mahdist."

"If the Mahdi himself were President of the Revolutionary Command Council, the military wouldn't be safe!"

"Sheikh Muhammad, you supported the military, and that's all there is to it. But we are waiting for the Guiding Imam to give his instruction. But we are not afraid, for we know that General Ja'far comes from an Ansarist family. And the Ansar will protect this country with their blood."

Muhammad Said laughed.

"You fool! There are Ansar and Khatmiyya there in Khartoum. Al-Azhari is in detention. Ahmad, the grandson of the Imam the Mahdi, is in detention. Here, anyone bringing us gasoline would be God's Mahdi and the grandson of the Prophet even if he was a communist. Our messages to the military will guarantee us gasoline. After you've harvested your dates, pray for the Mahdi or for Sayyid 'Ali al-Mirghani. There's no difference. We're farmers. Leave the political struggle to the efendis."

Someone else said, "You've almost turned into an efendi!"

"It's been an unusual time. The efendis in the thirties weren't like they are now. Or the military. Today our daughters are doctors. Who would have imagined it? The al-Nayir family has six female doctors, two of whom studied abroad. I'm a man who pees standing, not like women, if you'll excuse me. When the British chose me for Gordon

College, my father, may God have mercy on him," those present repeated the invocation, "refused, until the British ma'mur intervened. And he stopped Bashir from going to the Egyptian school in Tangasi. He said one is enough to be educated."

The al-Badri spokesman returned to the discussion, "We are Ansar! It is a belief and a religion. We are not afraid."

Muhammad Said laughed. "Leave off your lies, man! My father fought with the Mahdiyya. Then when it finished he joined the Khatmiyya again, as he had been before. If you don't know the history, ask your cousin, Hajj Hussein will tell you. All the house of al-Nayir fought in the Mahdiyya."

A sarcastic voice called out, "There's no doubt about that. But on which side?"

The gathering erupted in laughter but Muhammad Said wisely held his tongue and laughed with the others. Shigrib wasn't with them.

Al-Rashid made to leave without being noticed, just as he had come in. But his brother noticed him and called to him, "Is everything okay, Rashid?"

"Hajj Bashir and Hajj Hussein are supervising everything, sheikh, don't worry!"

"And the bridegroom?"

"Drowning in massage oil."

Muhammad Said sighed. "I wish we could drown in massage oil after being in this state."

Everyone laughed. They knew that the district sheikh and the most powerful man in the region wouldn't dare mention a second marriage except in jest. His wife, Hajja Radiya, frightened him more than anything else. But he was prone to joking, saying: "The man who doesn't fear his wife is not a man."

He pointed to his brother. "Come here, then. Are you looking for something?"

Rashid was caught off guard. Should he confess that he was looking for Abir? Looking for her magic, which turned hearts, and her pleasure, which she gave off like the whiff of scandal?

"I was looking for Ahmad Shigrib," he said quietly.

"Why?"

Before he could find a suitable lie, help arrived. People rushed outside and everyone started shouting.

"What's happening?"

"Have the young men started a fight?"

Someone rushed into the diwan and shouted, "Where is Shigrib?"

Muhammad Said told him off, "What's going on?"

"'Abd al-Razeq has been stung by a scorpion."

❦

Suleiman al-Hawati was the first to see Wazin al-Dahab when she arrived near the time of the afternoon prayer.

The woman had left the town of Al Dabba two days ago. She had made the journey to the north by begging for lifts from passers-by. She rode in a government Landrover from the town. Then she abandoned that to ride with some villagers from the village of Kallero, who gave her a ride on their donkeys. Then she waited on the bank of the river until she caught a boat that carried her for some distance. After that, she went up to the road to find a caravan to take her the short distance to Hajar Narti and completed her journey along the Nile until she could see Fayit Niddu's shack.

Suleiman al-Hawati was walking up the jetty from where the corpse had been tied up. He had checked again that it would have to be put up with for another day before it was buried. He was annoyed to have heard some people say he had made a mistake and that the corpse would start to decay if it was left for another day.

As he climbed the path, he looked up and found Fatima, the mother of the young girl, in front of him. Her face was tinged with sadness.

He knew she wouldn't answer but he said to her, "Come on, girl, why are you still so upset? You're killing yourself with grief. The drowned girl isn't your daughter and no corpse is going to appear after all this time. Go back to your family and seek refuge with them."

She turned her face from him without her eyes leaving the Nile.

"My girl, what's gone will not return. Your daughter is blessed. She is in paradise now."

Suleiman al-Hawati was speaking to the Nile and the waves replied. But Fatima did not answer him.

Silent as a severed palm trunk.

He shook his head in sorrow and was going to look for the bereaved woman when he noticed Dahab walking in the distance carrying her things on her head. She was swaying and her body was shaking as if she was walking on water.

He could mistake his wife from a distance like this but he couldn't mistake Dahab.

He was happy to see her. He forgot how he had got his way over leaving the corpse and shouted the good news to anyone in the shack, "Good news, everyone! Wazin al-Dahab has come!"

Fayit al-Niddu put out her head to look, as Suleiman greeted the returning woman with an embrace and took her things from her. Her sister smiled at her and they embraced, as people came out of the shack to greet the woman brought from far away by duty.

"It's been a long time, Dahab!"

"Happy returns, by God!"

"Welcome, welcome, Dahab! May the one who brought you bring us what you left behind!"

Dahab smiled as she was welcomed by both young and old. She was a slave, freed in her mid-fifties. If she didn't sing at a wedding, it was as though there hadn't been a wedding at all. If she didn't prepare a bride for a man, it was as though he had never known a woman. As for her record in giving men pleasure, that was something her family recalled with a smile but did not tell. It was said she was the one woman in the whole district who had tried British men. A British officer had fallen in love with her in her youth and had almost gone mad for her. But no one knew the truth exactly.

Her early marriage and her move to the town of Al Goled didn't stop her visiting Hajar Narti whenever someone asked for her or some business demanded her presence.

And for the wedding of 'Abd al-Hafez ibn al-Hussein al-Badri, she didn't need to wait for an invitation. She quickly sent a message announcing that she would come.

One of those greeting her shouted, "Your singing has brought us together. All we need is your sister's arak."

Dahab laughed. She was quite as nice as her sister. Her face had the sweetness of pure wine but her body was plump and quivered with fat. To praise her sister, she said, "You drink Fayit Niddu Walker and forget Wazin al-Dahab."

They laughed. Suleiman al-Hawati became excited and announced that he would escort her to the village on his donkey.

With his slim body and short frame, he ran quickly, untied his donkey from its stall and came back. Several people helped Dahab onto the donkey's back. Without complaining, the donkey bent his back and Dahab settled her things in her lap. She made a joke to those standing there and the donkey moved off with her and her escort.

The two of them joked together the whole way, smiling whenever they passed a group of villagers. As they passed some ghajar, Dahab called to them, and some of them turned. She pointed to one of them and cried, "Salih, ghajari? Are you still a thief?"

The ghajari's face broke into a smile. "Dahab! You're a good woman. What brought you to this evil village?"

Dahab's laughter rang out loud and Suleiman frowned. "Salih, these are my family. If I let them loose on you they would bury you alive."

Salih the ghajari replied mockingly, "God grants life... and God grants death!"

"Do you know the ghajari too?" Suleiman the fisherman asked her.

"They stayed with us in Dabba more than once. If they had a leader it would be this Salih. But they don't recognize any sheikhs or 'umdas. They are all equal."

Suleiman turned to look at the ghajari. He was tall, with an enormous protruding stomach. His eyes were colored like those of all his people and his skin was light colored, covered with dirt and grime.

"Dahab, you know the scorpion in its lair!"

She struck the back of his hand playfully and laughed. "And you, Suleiman, would fuck the scorpion in its sting."

His laughter rang out between the palm trees, which looked at them curiously. "Do you still remember, Dahab?"

"Have you forgotten when you volunteered to escort me?"

He smiled, and said, evasively, "Woman, I just wanted to do you a service. Is chivalry dead everywhere?"

"Remember chivalry, but don't look for me at night after the party!"

"Keep her with you, and I will come to you to look for her."

Dahab laughed until she almost slipped off the donkey's back. She clutched at Suleiman. "We're too old for all that, man! My oldest daughter gave birth three years ago. I'm a grandmother now. What do you want with old women?"

"Everything's possible, even fucking old women!"

This time, the palm trees couldn't conceal their laughter, as the pair burst into laughter until their tears flowed. As Suleiman wiped the tears from his face, he said, "I seek mercy from God, I seek mercy from almighty God! By God, it's been a long time, Dahab!"

She stretched out her hand to search in her things then withdrew it, holding a small plastic container, which she slipped to Suleiman from behind.

"Take this, a present for you. Arak, made from the best alcohol in Dabba."

He snatched the present and wrapped his cloak around it.

"Are you competing with Fayit Niddu now?"

"No, by God! But I hate to come with no presents for the family."

"The best present. Your sister only gets out her wine for important people first. Then what's left is given to people like me. A fisherman like me only gets the leftovers in a container."

She teased him, scolding him, "Are you complaining about my sister now?"

"I'll complain about her until I drink your wine then forget it."

Their conversation was interrupted by the women's ululations. They had reached the wedding venue. The place erupted at the sight of Wazin al-Dahab.

As soon as she got down, the drum was placed in her hand and people hovered around her to greet her. Without delay, she burst into song, beating on the drum as she did so.

> *Mother, sing for me,*
> *Tonight a traveler has come to you,*
> *Mother, sing for me,*
> *'Abd al-Hafez the tribesman.*

Suleiman watched her as she plunged into the crowds.

He smiled. He remembered an old story.

He sighed in longing. Then he took hold of her present and urged his donkey toward the corral.

❦

The cough had planted its arrowheads in Hajj Bashir's chest.

The world grew cloudy in his eyes and he leaned on the wall, trying hard not to let people see what was wrong with him. As the coughing came back to him, he covered his mouth with the sleeve of his cloak. When he drew it down, the sleeve was covered in blood.

In the morning, he had seen blood on the cloak he had been wearing the previous day. And here it was returning.

His body shook and trembled.

Was it sickness or fear?

He shut his eyes.

The sounds of singing came to him from afar. People moved around him as in a dream.

> *Come on, Mahjoub, get up and drive*
> *Leave Omdurman, hurry up and get going*
> *Let's see the beautiful woman of taste*
> *That all poetry falls short of describing.*

Was it someone singing in the courtyard, or was the singing in his head?

He was exhausted, as if he had walked from the ends of the earth. Now he felt what the horse had suffered.

That was about thirty years ago, but he had only understood it today.

His journey had been a very long one. Perhaps if he kept his eyes closed, he would find rest. Perhaps if he kept his eyes closed, he would see her.

Sukaina.

Are you here?

Sukaina.

"Hajj Bashir."

He stirred. He opened his eyes and saw a murky shadow standing in front of him. He was surprised to find himself sitting on the ground. He screwed up his eyes and saw Suleiman al-Hawati.

The fisherman was squatting in front of him.

"Are you okay, Hajj?"

"Fit as a fiddle!"

"You look exhausted. Your brow is furrowed."

He noticed the blood on his sleeve.

"Have you got a cut?"

"No. Perhaps it's from the blood of the animals. I'm okay. Just…"

His words were interrupted by a cough, and his body shook violently.

"Hajj, may God have mercy on you! See Ahmad Shigrib and get yourself examined. Your health is worth everything. Forget 'Abd al-Hafez's wedding and get some rest, Hajj!"

Hajj Bashir stretched out his hand and leaned on Suleiman's shoulder as he got up with determination. As he struggled to stand, he called with certainty upon the righteous sheikhs and put his trust in the saints.

"Sidi al-Hasan!"

Suleiman al-Hawati helped him pull himself up.

"The sheikhs of the Warariq will be with you and help you, Hajj!"

He collected himself. He thought she had been near him then gone away. For a moment he thought he had glimpsed her walking into the distance. But the woman he was looking at stood close to the light of the lamp and he could see her clearly. It was not at all like her, it could not be her.

"That's enough, Hawati! Come on, see what's going on behind you, man! I am fine."

Suleiman muttered in protest. But he was not going to argue with Hajj Bashir. And Dahab's booze hiding in his clothes was screaming out in its search for a companion.

Hajj Bashir left his place fighting a headache. He walked in search of a drinking companion and found 'Abd al-Razeq in front of him. "You're in luck!" he said.

As he revealed his treasure, 'Abd al-Razeq's face lit up.

"Fayit Niddu's arak?"

"No, something even more tempting and deadly! Dahab's arak, all the way from Dabba!"

'Abd al-Razeq cried out, "God be blessed!"

Then he looked around him and asked, "Alone or in a group?"

"There are not enough people to make a group. If we go away from people, we can drink enough to satisfy us."

"Come on, I'll show you somewhere nearby, where no one will disturb us."

They walked into the house. Suleiman al-Hawati thought that 'Abd al-Razeq would head for the open ground to avoid other people. But he walked with him through the crowded courtyard, then went in behind the water pitchers. Between the pitchers and the wall there was a damp, narrow corridor, at the end of which was a dark open space that was out of sight. A suitable hiding place.

The two men jumped when they heard a sudden movement. They could not be seen from there. "In the name of God, the merciful, the compassionate! Who's that?" shouted 'Abd al-Razeq.

He saw two dark lumps separating from one another. One of them raced off, collided with him, passed him, and fled. The second dark lump stood still.

Suleiman approached it cautiously. "Man or jinn?"

With his face almost touching her, he saw it was Abir.

He laughed and called to his companion, "It's Fayit Niddu's daughter!"

"Arak is stealthy, Abir!"

The two men laughed.

"Who's the brave man that left you and fled?"

The girl didn't answer but stayed where she was, as if she had been expecting them. 'Abd al-Razeq gestured at her to leave. She slipped silently between them and went away.

Suleiman al-Hawati shot a glance at her fragrance, as if she had left behind her a path of light. And 'Abd al-Razeq beat his chest with the back of his hand to wake himself. "O man!"

Suleiman smiled. "Tell me if the girl doesn't arouse you the same way she does the whole village!"

"I take refuge with God," 'Abd al-Razeq replied reproachfully. "Fuck the two holes in hell, man! I slept with her mother, so she's forbidden to me till Judgment Day!"

"That's for free women, man! With slaves, there's nothing like that!"

"No, my brother. It's better to keep away from suspicion. It's absolutely forbidden!"

Suleiman took out his alcohol. "You and your religious law," he said. "Where shall we sit?"

'Abd al-Razeq slipped off his shoe and tested the ground. It was damp from the water from the jars. He stepped forward a little until he felt a place that was dry. "Here," he said to his companion.

Suleiman positioned his short, slim body elegantly on the ground, while 'Abd al-Razeq leaned down slowly. He put his palm flat on the ground, leaned on it then relaxed his body backwards. He sat down with his bottom directly above the scorpion that stung him; and it stung him there.

Abir emerged from behind the water jars to the noise of the crowded courtyard.

Her aunt's voice filled the place.

> Come to me, you who moisten my dry days,
> Come to me, you who moisten my dry days.

She passed quickly through the crowds and noticed Ahmad Shigrib. The medical assistant had been looking for her since sunset. He had found her, but he was no luckier than Rashid when he found her.

He had wanted the young girl more than Rashid. She had been with him in the morning, and yesterday afternoon as well. And Shigrib was cleverer than him at looking in places he did not think of. That was how he had seen her following a youth to the narrow corridor behind the water jars.

His heart skipped a beat. But he consoled himself that she would be his soon. He knew that the village youths were all keen on her and he couldn't stop that. He would wait until this filthy young man had finished, then he would run away with her from the wedding venue to the surgery.

He deceived himself by saying that he was saving her, and that he was not like the others. He believed in freedom and equality. He didn't believe that a man should have control over a woman.

She would emerge from behind the water jars in a moment and he would help her escape to the surgery from the exploitation of the other men and youths. There they would be two equal human beings. She would be free between his arms. He would save her, like a skilled swimmer saving a drowning woman from the sea of men's desires.

Ahmad Shigrib was not a communist in the full sense of the term but he was close to the Left. He had grown bored with Khartoum after the Communist Party takeover more than three years ago. And he had escaped death the day the angry Islamists and Ansar al-Mahdi, together with the enraged mobs, had pursued the Communists on the streets, charging them with insulting Aisha, the Prophet's wife.

The nationalist Ismail al-Azhari, the President of the Command Council, the man who raised the flag of independence, promised the angry mobs who surrounded his house that he would stand up to the corruption of the Communists and Communism. The parties that Shigrib would not dare call reactionary in front of the people of Hajar Narti rushed in, took the place of the Communist party, and drove its representatives from Parliament.

Communism became an offence.

After that, Shigrib embarked on a journey to seek his salvation. An opportunity to work in the surgery in a faraway village he had never heard of before came to him like a magic solution. He could be a communist in Hajar Narti, but only if he respected the sectarian beliefs of the people and their party allegiances.

He picked up his books and his thoughts, said goodbye to his mother. and fled north to Hajar Narti.

He spent a year and a half in the quiet, humble village. A year and a half in which his communism was nothing except an expression he had written on the surgery wall to remind him of who he was. "Long live the struggle of the working class! Long live the struggle of the people!"

Against whom?

Things seemed complicated here. He didn't know how to distinguish clearly between the bourgeois feudalists and the working class. Who were "the people" in Hajar Narti? What he was certain of was that they were all reactionary. They believed in sectarianism and religious rule. But they didn't seem to be enemies. They were kind and gentle and loved gossip. Were these people his enemies?

The one thing that saved him from himself was the sight of Abir dancing at the circumcision party of al-Azhari, Hajj Bashir's son.

A child, slim and dark, with no legal father, no shoes, and hair untidy as a forest of thorns.

He said to himself, "This child is a victim."

But his soul was led astray by the young girl.

He struggled with himself for a long time. A year and a half, more than five hundred days, in fact. But when Abir threw the fruits of the succulent doum tree from the edge of her dress and came toward him, she wiped out all the previous days.

Here he was now, the medical assistant, the leftist fleeing from the struggles of power and parties. He was standing in the courtyard of Hajj Hussein al-Badri's house, amid the crowds celebrating the wedding of one of the ruling class, waiting for a young man who was still an adolescent to finish so he could take his girlfriend away to where they could be alone.

But as soon as the youth appeared from his hiding place behind the jars, another youth went in past him!

Shigrib, waiting in his place there, counted three young men, the last of them running away as Suleiman al-Hawati and 'Abd al-Razeq came in.

Before his heart could melt, mercy came to him. He saw the young girl calmly come out, walking as though she had not been doing what he knew she had.

Their eyes met.

His eyes were wide as a raging river. Her eyes were dead as a deserted house.

Three young men, Abir?

One after the other?

Won't you choose one?

Had she chosen him when the doum fell from her dress, or was he just like them?

Did the answer matter to him now?

He was about to walk toward her, to take her before she was taken by another adolescent.

He was about to... He got ready to wave to her. But 'Abd al-Razeq's shout cut through the darkness behind the water jars, landing in the middle of the wedding courtyard and terrifying everyone.

❦

She was dancing like a ban tree stalk, swaying with the wind. Whenever she bent her slim body, empty of any furrow or bulge, everyone was aroused and the young men whistled. She had in her something like the Night of Power. You could feel it but not see it. You knew it but your hands did not possess it. It was there, but what was it?

❦

Muhammad Said arrived at the head of the group of frightened men. He moved sluggishly, weighed down by his enormous body, fifty-three years, and the gravity of his position. He was followed by the leading people of the village and guests. They were greeted by Suleiman al-Hawati, carrying the stung body of 'Abd al-Razeq with some help from the others.

'Abd al-Razeq was making a noise like a cow in labor. Behind them, one of the hangers-on was carrying the dead scorpion. It was black, the length of a thumb, and crushed, after being trampled by 'Abd al-Razeq's rescuers. But it had been too quick for them and had already released its poison in 'Abd al-Razeq.

"Make way, people! Don't stop him getting air!" Hajj Bashir shouted, between the coughing and the crowd.

"Where's Shigrib?" someone called out.

The medical assistant extracted himself from his love trap, he tried to put Abir from his mind but she wouldn't leave. He came forward in a state of confusion to examine the man who had been stung.

"Take him to the surgery."

'Abd al-Razeq was dripping with sweat and snorting as he tried to catch his breath.

As they hurried him to the surgery, the wedding venue was thrown into confusion. 'Abd al-Hafez raised himself from his bed and hurried out barefoot, the henna on his feet mingling with the sand. When the news reached the women in the kitchen, they hurried out. His two wives wailed and Dahab's dallouka fell silent. There was only the sound of the tambour in the distance, where the news had not yet reached the crowd.

Hussein al-Badri took aside some of his people, Muhammad Said in their midst.

"What do you think?"

"It's in God's hands, but it's quite simple, Shigrib will treat him."

"The party has broken up, and a lot of people have followed 'Abd al-Razeq to the surgery."

"The people that have gone will come back. We have guests!"

"Should we serve supper and end the henna party?"

"It's not the first or the last sting we've had," said Muhammad Said firmly. "We owe a duty to our guests. Shut the weeping women up and let Dahab return to her singing. 'Abd al-Razeq is our patient and we will look after him. The party will go on and the henna ceremony will go on."

"A good decision, Sheikh!"

"The wisdom of someone who knows how to behave!"

As the men dispersed, they chased away the women. "What's this sassy behavior! Are you doctors? Go back to the kitchen!" Hajja Radiya shouted.

Nur al-Sham muttered something about the need to support 'Abd al-Razeq's wives, who were hurrying behind their husband.

"Your duty now is the kitchen!"

Fayit Niddu gave an order to carry on serving the rice. Al-Hussein al-Badri slapped a female mourner who would not be quiet and someone ordered Dahab to sing.

Muhammad Said led the guests into the diwan.

"It's okay, everyone. A trivial matter. Help yourselves, help yourselves!"

In only a few moments, things had calmed down. Perhaps a third of those present went to the surgery but the courtyard was still packed as 'Abd al-Hafez returned to his place. The old women hurried to wipe off the henna mixed with sand from his feet, and started to put on a new batch, invoking the name of God and suppressing their tears.

Dahab's *dallouka* rang out. Some of the girls clapped tensely with her, then the slave girl's voice rang out:

Paradise of paradise
Where have you been, Mambo?
A lovers' paradise
Mambo.

Gradually, the effect of the incident abated, except for some face-tious comments among a few people hovering here and there. But the commotion gave Rashid his prey at last.

❦

In the darkness after supper, among the empty houses, with the sound of the party coming from afar, people hurried 'Abd al-Razeq to the surgery. At their head was his companion Suleiman, who was consumed by fear.

The village was silent as a deserted campsite. No light. No sound.

They took him into the surgery, where Shigrib lit a lamp, and they put him on the bed. Relatives and hangers-on crammed into the narrow room. Shigrib had learned not to turn people away at an examination.

To gather with a sick person was considered a duty, and to crowd around him a form of support. But Hajj Bashir—who had come late after calling in at his own house—told them off until the room was empty. Only he and Suleiman and 'Abd al-Razeq's two wives remained, together with one of his cousins.

Shigrib rummaged around in his scanty medicines, while Hajj Bashir took a piece of coal out of his pocket. "Take this!" He said to the medical assistant. "This is scorpion's rock, it sucks the poison from the body in seconds!"

He had come after the crowd because he had called in at his own house to bring the cure, but Shigrib ignored him, hoping to find something useful in his ill-supplied medicine cupboards. But his search failed.

He struggled a little then gave in.

With the help of the men, he turned 'Abd al-Razeq on his face, lifted his cloak and pulled his trousers down. 'Abd al-Razeq was shaking like a flare.

With a razor he cut the site of the sting. Thick black blood appeared, and the scorpion's rock was put on it. The coal-like rock would draw the poison from the body of the bitten man. But it needed constant watching.

It would be a long night.

Shigrib thought of his misfortune. A stray scorpion had let Abir escape from him. If it weren't for the scorpion, the girl would be with him now.

But instead of the girl's body, he would spend the night watching 'Abd al-Razeq's behind in the company of his two fearful, crying wives.

※

Many a scorpion has cured a man's lust!

In the heart of the commotion, Rashid stretched out his hand and clasped Abir's palm. He didn't look at her. He stood beside her, looking with the crowd at 'Abd al-Razeq's body as it was brought out from behind the water jars. While his brother, Hajj Bashir, gave his orders, Rashid was pulling at Abir's palm, but she didn't lift her eyes to him.

As people moved toward the surgery, he pulled her away, slipping through the crowd. Taking advantage of the fear and curiosity of those leaving, he smuggled her away from the wedding venue. As if the crowd were escorting his passion with invocations and tears.

In the darkness of the quiet paths, he escaped from the others with Abir in his grasp—as if they had had an appointment for a thousand years.

She didn't run away or hesitate, and the pair walked on silently until they were out of the way. When he was sure they had escaped from anyone watching, he sighed.

"At last, daughter of jinn!"

She was barefoot. Her hand in his was thin and bony but it was warm. He stretched his hand out to fondle her back as they walked to his house.

If he had wanted to compare her to something, he would have said she was a thin ewe.

Her body was slim. He fondled it but he could feel no bumps and his hand did not sink into fat. But although he could not see her, she aroused his lust in the darkness.

"What's your secret, girl?"

She handed him her silence. If he had dragged his donkey by its halter it would have resisted him before obeying. But Abir walked with him, unconcerned. If he walked her to his house, she would go. If he had pushed her into the mosque well, she would have sunk without a sound.

"Aren't you afraid?"

Her voice was like that of a child.

"My mother says my heart is dead."

He stretched out his hand searching for her left breast. A ripe lemon, no bigger.

"Your heart is here. It is beating."

They reached his house. He pushed her gently between the two halves of the open door and went in behind her. They passed through the wide courtyard.

In the darkness, the outline of the house appeared enormous. An outside diwan and a building with four rooms. At the far end of the courtyard, not visible to someone entering, was a kitchen, and a small side door leading to the pen and the lavatory.

His brother, Muhammad Said al-Sheikh, had built this house for him ten years ago. As soon as he reached twenty, he had had the idea that he was ready for marriage. But he made his house a place for continual wine and evening gatherings with his light-hearted friends.

Most of them had married and remembered these evening gatherings. As for him, he followed his brother Hajj Bashir during the day, and at night drank arak with his companions.

Where would he find time for marriage?

He was not preoccupied with women. In his thirty-one years, he had tried seven women, no more. Three of them were servants, four adventurous village girls, or girls eager to please him in the hope that he would embark on marriage with someone who could satisfy him.

Abir tonight would be the eighth experience in his life. And he suspected that she would probably be the eighth experience for just this night. The girl would provide no satisfaction and didn't say no to anyone who asked.

It was summertime and the rooms of the house, built of mud brick, were very hot. There was no time to open windows or doors.

He dragged the girl toward the men's outside diwan. They entered blindly. He fumbled around until he found a rolled-up bed, laid it out, and pushed the girl onto it.

The sound of his breathing in the darkness was like a howling wind, exuding desire. He was about to catch fire and light the place up.

He could not see the girl. But her mere presence filled him with lust like a flood.

He embraced her and kissed her impetuously. Wherever his lips fell, he licked.

He played with her body and she played with his excitement.

When he lost his senses and he found himself flying in the air as he tried to touch the ceiling, she suddenly pushed him off her.

He was completely taken by surprise. "Are you mad?" he cried.

Her voice crept through the darkness, brittle from lack of use.

"Before you do what you want, I demand a promise from you."

He groped for her tensely with his hand.

"What promise, you wretched girl? Come here!"

He heard the sound of her moving and stretched out a hand but she slipped away from him. The steed of desire carried him away. Losing control, he shouted, "I will promise you anything, everything, come here!"

He seized her hand in the darkness. She moved with the confidence of a cat. "Promise me that you will be my mediator with Hajja Radiya."

There was no possibility of going back, as he embarked on his act of madness. He promised her.

And so his tally of women reached eight.

Daylight flooded Hajar Narti.

A tense Tuesday, after the previous night. People had got up early to visit the surgery to check on 'Abd al-Razeq. The man himself had returned from half-way down the road to destruction after a night of convulsions, fever, and vomiting. Shigrib had stayed up with him, mixing his medicine with the coal-stone scorpion cure.

People were piled up in front of the surgery—men, women, and children. This story would live a long time and would be mixed with gossip. "On 'Abd al-Hafez al-Badri's henna night, 'Abd al-Razeq was stung." The story would be chopped and changed about, so that imagined details were added and the facts of what actually happened fell away. In gossip, it didn't matter what happened. What mattered was that the story should be entertaining when it was told.

People came in in groups, and whenever a group left, another one took its place.

"Penance, man!"

"The evil has passed. God has cured you."

"God grant you health, man. Be brave!"

Some of them took advantage of their presence in the surgery to ask Ahmad Shigrib for a cure for some pain or other.

When a group of women came in, they embraced 'Abd al-Razeq's two wives and wept.

"May God ordain his recovery!"

"He'll get up for you healthy, God willing!"

"Health and wealth!"

Nur al-Sham plucked up her courage and asked, inquisitively, "'Abd al-Razeq! I hope you recover, God willing! Where did the scorpion sting you?"

The men said nothing but exchanged glances and smiles.

The woman insisted, with genuine interest, "Where did the scorpion sting you?"

'Abd al-Razeq replied curtly, "Behind the water jars."

Another woman interrupted, to clarify what she thought was a misunderstanding, "Yes, we know. But where?"

Suleiman al-Hawati hid his laughter as 'Abd al-Razeq repeated, "Behind the water jars."

"We know. I'm asking where it stung you!" Nur al-Sham repeated, confused.

When he could help it no more, Suleiman burst out laughing, while Shigrib turned his face to the wall to hide his laughter. The two wives said nothing from embarrassment.

"I told you, woman, behind the jars! That's all there is to it!"

The women cowered in front of him as he shouted and drew closer to each other as if to protect one another. Embarrassed, they made their apologies. "May God decree your recovery! Don't be angry!" Then they went out, taking with them their questions and their criticism of the man for his nervousness.

After doing their duty visiting the stung man, groups of people made their way in several boats to do their duty at the wedding venue.

The men exchanged whispers about what had happened to Nur al-Sham's question and laughed under their breath, while the women tried to deduce the place of the sting. One of them claimed that 'Abd al-Razeq had suffered the same fate as one of his in-laws in the nearby village of al-Konj, when a scorpion stung him on his penis and he died.

Nur al-Sham struck her chest in fright. "Oh, the shame of it!"

She blamed herself for the temerity of her question. She wished she could have interrogated her husband instead of this scandal. But Hajj Bashir had only come back home at dawn and left quickly at sunrise for his brother's house. He didn't have time for questions.

Nur al-Sham's question would be immortalized in gossip. Whenever the wedding of 'Abd al-Hafez al-Badri was mentioned the men would talk about 'Abd al-Razeq, who was stung by a scorpion "behind the water jars."

✿

The two brothers met for tea in the morning in Muhammad Said al-Sheikh's diwan.

They looked quite different. Hajj Bashir was tall but had grown thinner over the last few months, while Sheikh Muhammad was fat. There was no more than two years age difference between them. But the formalities of respect between them were extreme. Hajj Bashir treated his elder brother with the utmost deference. Rashid, who was two decades younger than them, had grown up in the shadow of that relationship of theirs; they looked after him like fathers, and he respected them like a besotted disciple.

Muhammad Said could hardly do anything in the village without consulting Hajj Bashir. The city had stolen his three sons from him and the universities had swallowed them up. He had no companion left except his brother, his confidant and mainstay.

Muhammad Said sensed danger.

The country was changing. It wasn't the first period of military rule. Two years after the departure of the British, the military had seized power, but were then forced to abdicate it. Then they returned again before six years were out. But he felt it was different this time. He was following the radio, and telegrams were coming from Khartoum. These were not elderly officers like last time. They were hot-tempered youths who talked about communism and socialism. This was only their third day in power but he knew that the country would change forever.

He didn't reveal his fears to anyone. If they talked to him about the coup, he expressed his contempt for the matter.

"Coups, the military, and politics are there in Khartoum. Here in Hajar Narti we are only concerned with gasoline for agriculture. Let them do what they want there."

But with his brother he hid nothing.

"These people have come to stay, Bashir. They will see us—'umdas, notables, leading men of the village—only as enemies."

Hajj Bashir sipped his tea with milk, filling himself with its delicious smell. "Do you think they will snatch power from us in favor of the al-Badri family?" he asked.

"The issue is bigger than Hajar Narti. Bigger than the 'umda's position and that of the the district sheikh. They want to change everything. The demon of power and the recklessness of youth will tempt them to change everything. After all the telegrams of support, they will now ask people to go out and demonstrate in support of them. They will want expressions of complete loyalty and submission. No one asks for that unless they have big plans."

"Things don't stay as they are for long. They will go just as they came."

Muhammad Said looked at him for a time, contemplating how his body had grown thin and how exhausted he looked. His brother was ill, there was no doubt about that, but he was still stubborn. Perhaps it was the illness that was keeping him from seeing the oncoming danger.

"They are a flood, Bashir, a flood that will sweep away everything. We will all drown. The whole country will drown. I don't think there is any escape for us."

"Perhaps you are exaggerating their power, sheikh!"

Muhammad Said said nothing. He hoped he was wrong.

"We will see."

Then he suddenly changed the subject.

"Should we bury the girl's body today?"

"No one knows where she came from. And she can't wait longer than that. I'll send Rashid and Suleiman to bury her after the noon prayer."

"A body no one knows where it came from. And a country with fate unknown. What times we live in!"

"They are joyful times, sheikh! Tomorrow is the birthday of the Prophet, and on Thursday people will arrive from Khartoum to celebrate the wedding. Let's just follow the events, one at a time."

"We can't do anything else."

He fiddled with his stick. "Did Rashid ever mention the wedding to you?"

Hajj Bashir smiled. "No, he runs away if you mention it to him. But he's still young. Let him enjoy his feckless youth for a little."

"He's over thirty! By his age, I'd had two children. And you were married to your deceased wife."

"Times are not what they used to be."

"I wish they were!"

"It's the way life is."

"That's the only thing that frightens me. If changing times were a rare thing, it wouldn't bother me. But it's the way life is. It's a real event, without a doubt."

"God's command. If we're patient, we will heal. And God's command will prevail. And if we're not patient, and we act as unbelievers, God's command will still prevail."

"All good things come from God. With His blessing, I will carry out what I have planned for today; then let us break our fast in the wedding venue and make preparations for the Eve of the Mawlid tomorrow."

"God willing!"

Hajj Bashir got up with difficulty and his brother gave him a look of pity. "Look after your health, Bashir!"

He smiled. "God's command will prevail, sheikh!"

Muhammad Said's heart shrank. But he restrained himself from replying. He looked into the distance to see his other fears beckoning to him.

He believed that evil days were approaching, and that the country would certainly drown.

Nothing will be enough for the evil of the military. But it is all we can do.

When the 'umda Said al-Nayir died at the beginning of 1939, Muhammad Said had only one year of study left in the Teachers' Faculty at Gordon College.

The telegram that reached him wasn't the news of his father's death but a family order to travel quickly to Hajar al-Narti to take on the position of 'umda.

He needed a little time to appreciate the meaning of the message. "Come quickly. The British will give the position of 'umda to al-Badri. You are needed urgently, to inherit your right."

That is how he found out about his father's death.

When he disembarked from the steamship his five uncles were waiting for him. Messages from the British followed, ordering that a decision be taken on the post of 'umda.

He found authority waiting for him, as well as a wife. Those were troubled days. He had left behind him groups of graduates who formed a political club that brought them together to demand independence for the country. The world was on fire as it awaited a war that was beckoning in the distance. He turned his back on all that and returned to Hajar Narti to become 'umda and marry Radiya, his cousin.

Negotiations with the British, warding off the conspiracies of the al-Badri family, accepting authority, and marriage consumed him from inside. He only visited his father's grave after several weeks, a few days before the birth of his brother Rashid.

When he looked back on those days thirty years later, he felt a little nostalgic and extremely regretful.

Why hadn't he refused to give up his studies? Why hadn't he left the post of 'umda to the al-Badri family or to his brother, who was hopelessly in love with a married woman? Why had he married Radiya, as if he was a girl with no mind of her own?

He hadn't asked for his cousin and she hadn't accepted. They had simply been told to get married so they did.

They expected them to have children—so they did.

Only two years after his return, he was totally immersed in the affairs of Hajar Narti, as 'umda, husband, and father. His life in Khartoum, his studies under his British teachers, his involvement in politics, his independence, and his attempts to write poetry, all seemed like a dream. A dream in someone else's sleep.

His dream of being a poet in the capital had come to an end and his future as an efendi disappeared. The future that the British ma'mur had pressed upon him and his father had convinced him of was gone. The sons of leading men must study to become the efendis of the Sudanese administration of the country. He had thrown away that future and put on a gown and cloak and large turban.

Had he been unable to say no?

He had listened to the instructions of his uncles and felt he had a duty to obey. He had no right to refuse. It wouldn't be proper for him to refuse. Refusal would be a betrayal of his duty to his family, to his heritage, and to the whole way he had been brought up.

They made him 'umda, so he became 'umda.

They made him marry, so he married.

They made him assume authority, so he took it on his shoulders and fired.

He didn't appear weak, but his dominating cousin read his submissiveness in their first days together. Radiya had power and a wicked nature—as if she was a shadow of her grandmother al-Afiya. She thought of their marriage as a necessary family imposition and undertook it faithfully in the extreme. She was hewn from the same mountain as her uncles. Traditions, the family, and authority were everything.

Radiya saw him being given orders and obeying submissively. He did not appear to be sincere nor proud. He did not take the initiative but merely followed in the family's footsteps.

She could not accept such behavior from him. She thought him weak. And when she was unable to make him a believer like herself, she freed herself from the submissiveness of being a wife and bore a burden that was more appropriate for him.

He had been made to bear the trust so he bore it. But it was Radiya who embraced it and defended it and fought for thirty years to protect it. She was like the flood and the wind and the fires in the palms—a force to sweep everything away as she defended the heritage and authority of the house of al-Nayir.

She despised slaves, male or female. She tamed disobedient wives, stirred up men, circumcised both boys and girls, and rebuked frivolous youths.

If change was the habit of life, Radiya was the Jebel Barkal to challenge that habit.

Now Muhammad Said wished he had been like her. Perhaps he would have been able to ward off what was coming.

᪥

A little after noon, Rashid and Suleiman al-Hawati buried the corpse of the drowned girl.

They took it in Suleiman's boat to a spot not far away, then dug a hole in the mud beside the Nile and buried the corpse there.

When they had finished they heard Fatima, the child's mother's voice ring out like a wall of rock being split in two.

Here was another corpse being buried when Su'ad was still unburied.

᪥

"The handsome man has come… The handsome man has come."

That was how the people heard the sound of the bus's horn when the driver Mahjoub drove it into the village. He would make the horn sing and dance, and the boys would run behind him and sing with it. "The handsome man has come… The handsome man has come."

Mahjoub would arrive exactly on time on Thursday afternoon. He had been the driver for more than thirty-five years. The journey from the capital took two and a half days through the heart of the desert.

A long journey across the vast wilderness. The bus would be driving gracefully through the sand, then disaster would strike and it would sink solidly into it. Then the passengers would get out, push the bus, run behind it, and board it again as it struggled to free its wheels from the sand trap.

When they alighted at the last stop, the village mosque, the passengers seemed as alike as sets of miserable twins. They were covered in dust so that their faces couldn't be seen, heads coated in earth as if they had just emerged from their graves. The two-and-a-half-day journey had extinguished every trace of the comforts of the city.

They would disembark with ugly faces, cracked lips, and bleary eyes. But everyone who came, at whatever time or occasion, confirmed that arriving at the village was worth all they had suffered. Some of them would go further and assert that the hard journey had cleansed them of the city smoke to enjoy the paradise of the village.

People would greet them with water for washing and embraces of welcome.

A long hug, tears of joy, and repeated words of welcome.

"Thank God for your safe arrival!"

"Blessings, good to see you!"

"Praise God that we see you safe and well!"

"May God keep you safe, may God bless you!"

The whole village gathered together and no one stayed behind. As they greeted the newcomers who had traveled to the wedding across the desert, their cases were carried in random fashion; every door was open to the newcomers, and every house became a place to stay. When the traveler reached his residence, the children were sent to look for his bags. A red bag would emerge from one house and go into another. A cardboard box with the name of its owner in large letters would be carried from one house to the next, and a boy would carry a white plastic bucket at a run to where its owner was staying.

By around the time of the sunset prayer, every traveler had found his things, and after a good wash, their faces could be seen in the light of the lamps.

People went around the houses once again to greet the newcomers, as if to check the identities of those they had met after they had shaken the earth off and rubbed the dust off their faces.

"Thank God for your safe arrival!" they repeated yet again.

"Blessings, good to see you!"

"Praise God that we see you safe and well!"

"May God keep you safe, may God bless you!"

If it hadn't been the time of the wedding, fatir with laban would have been served for supper to the travelers. But it was a special occasion, and just after the celebration of the Prophet's Birthday. So roast meat and broth had been prepared and needed people to eat it.

The village turned into an open feast. The singers—as well as people from every part of the region and neighboring villages—waited for supper to end so that the great henna night could begin.

The newcomers smiled at the whole village. On special occasions, there was no difference between the al-Badri and the al-Nayir families, or between the other houses and families. On such occasions, Hajar al-Narti all became one family again, with one common ancestor, just as it had started hundreds of years ago.

Muhammad Said asked some of the efendis for news from the capital.

"The world has been turned upside down."

"Detentions every day; declarations from the Revolutionary Command Council. But people are optimistic."

"This village needs strength!"

"The Ansar are preparing something. Things will not go smoothly. But God forbid the military, Communists, or nationalists take over the village."

As everyone crowded into the courtyard of Hajj Hussein al-Badri's wedding venue, the conical loudspeakers vibrated. The people called them "elephant's ears" and they gave out a disturbing whistle. Then the sound of the tambour rang out, accompanied by the rhythmic beats of the drum.

The voice of the singer rose up:

That handsome man is by nature always calm and serene
Tell me more of his attributes, intoxicate me, singer,
The gazelle in the valley is shy of the wide-eyed ones
And the cheek, like flowers, you will always find dewy.

Only at this point did Fayit Niddu break the seals of her store of hidden wine. The glasses went around, accompanied by trilling sounds of joy.

✺

A night like this was among the hardest for Hajja Radiya.

A night that challenged her puritanical attitudes and forced her to compromise a little with ill-mannered idiots, as she called them. Wine, dancing, and boys chasing girls into the wilderness and shady places.

She usually escaped by hiding away in the kitchen, carefully supervising the service, and chasing the slaves. But tonight she was happy to leave her hiding place to show Shahinaz off in front of everyone.

She left behind her primness and went out proudly, to take her around the women. She trilled for her when she tried to imitate the dancing of the village girls to the strains of the tambour. When some of the boys saw the girl and tried to whistle, she gave them a sideways look, so their voices died on their lips. She was proud of her, forgiving of her youthful arrogance and flirtatiousness.

Mahjoub's bus had brought from Khartoum the seventeen-year-old fruit of the al-Nayir family. When she alighted from the bus, she was neat and tidy as if she had just made herself up. Amid the grubbiness of the other arrivals, she looked a proper color.

Shahinaz was the daughter of Hajja Radiya's brother. She had been born in the capital and still lived there. She only knew the village through visiting on special occasions.

When she came for holidays, all the boys volunteered to wait on her. They would climb palm trees for her and steal ripe dates, invade the mango groves and pluck the best fruit.

She wasn't particularly pretty, and her harsh features were perhaps rather like those of her aunt Radiya. But the easy life of the city had clothed her in a certain elegance. Since her childhood she had shone and sparkled as if she were the planet Venus. Her clothes were clean and starched, and her behavior became more polished as she developed. She looked at the world, when she looked at it at all, as a young princess.

She was spoiled and loved by her aunt, and all the al-Nayir family loved her for that reason.

That was the first of Abir's curses.

Ever since Fayit Niddu's pregnancy had become apparent after that summer night with 'Abd al-Hafez, she had wanted to be blessed with a girl.

She avoided Hajja Radiya, and tried to avoid her pregnancy becoming apparent to that prim woman. But her heart was attached to the young Shahinaz.

Before she was four, she visited Hajar Narti and all the houses welcomed her. Her aunt's husband, Muhammad Said, picked her up, lifted her high, and composed some poetry for her:

> I was pleased, and shaken so hard
> In your eyes is beauty, Shahinaz

Fayit Niddu fled from Hajja Radiya's sight, but she watched the young girl. She promised herself that if she was blessed with the girl she wanted, she would call her Shahinaz and she would be a doctor.

She hid that promise as she had hidden her pregnancy.

Then, when she was betrayed by her stomach and the village gossip, Hajja Radiya found out that "the servant in the 'umda's courtyard is pregnant."

Radiya seethed like a sky teeming with shooting stars. She seized Fayit Niddu by her short coarse hair and beat her almost to death. She dragged her along the ground, shouting, "You whore! You disgraceful servant. You bastard. Is a bastard to inflict another bastard on us?"

She slapped her, kicked her, and bit her in anger.

Fayit Niddu withdrew into herself. She didn't resist but she protected her belly with her hands. Hajja Radiya twice tried to kick her unborn child but Fayit Niddu took the kicks on her arms, which were crossed in front of her swollen belly.

Hajja Radiya shouted madly, "You'll lose this wretched pregnancy."

Fayit Niddu pleaded with her, asking for mercy. Muhammad Said interceded for her, as did Hajj Bashir and his wife, Sukaina bint al-Badri, and all those who had influence with Radiya.

The old woman softened, after she had sworn that no more bastards would be born from the 'umda's courtyard.

To fulfil her promise, Hajj Bashir swore, "We'll send her to her sister Dahab in al-Dabba. She can give birth there and you will fulfil your oath."

Hajja Radiya reluctantly accepted. And so the bastard would not be born in Hajar Narti. But she exploited Fayit Niddu's pregnancy to launch a violent attack on all the loose slaves and girls in the village. She followed and watched them so that anyone seeking their pleasure became afraid that Hajja Radiya might catch them and the barking dogs betray them.

Fayit Niddu was sent south to her sister, and stayed with her for more than two months. When she returned she was carrying her dark-skinned daughter and a birth certificate giving her name as Shahinaz.

The village stories don't exactly explain why Fayit Niddu did such a stupid thing as though she didn't know the consequences. Some women say that she liked Hajja Radiya's niece a lot and wanted her daughter to have luck like hers, so she called her that as a good omen. Some swore that she did it to anger the old woman. And others attributed it to the natural stupidity of slaves.

Whatever the reason, the return of Fayit Niddu carrying her baby scandalized the village. If Hajar Narti had woken and found the Nile flowing to the south, or the shrines of the Warariq sheikhs flying in the air, it wouldn't have made an impression like the earthquake occasioned by the naming.

Hajja Radiya swore that she would kill the infant, but she was grabbed by the other women as she sank her claws into Fayit Niddu to snatch her baby from her.

"Hajja, blessings be on the Prophet!"

"Seek guidance from God, Hajja Radiya!"

"Seek forgiveness and curse the Devil!"

Radiya did not curse him but she swore by him, by Sayyid Hasan al-Mirghani, the Warariq sheikhs, her father's grave, and her mother's breasts that she would kill her.

As she struggled with the women in Fayit Niddu's room to escape and seize the slave and her child, a shadow fell over them. They heard the voice of Muhammad Said thundering at the door of the room.

"What's going on here?"

Fayit Niddu fled with her baby into a faraway corner. The women cowered, for they had detected the ring of anger in the respected man's voice.

Radiya stood alone in the middle of the room gasping for breath. Her breathing sounded like the thumping of the Project's irrigation machine. She was bursting with anger and her red eyes lit up the room. But when she looked into her husband's sullen face she froze.

They briefly exchanged glowering looks, until, with unaccustomed harshness, he asked her, "Radiya, What is going on?"

Their looks wrestled with each other, until the woman replied, in a strangled voice, "Ask the whore her daughter's name!"

Muhammad Said shifted his gaze to Fayit Niddu, who sat in her corner, consumed by fear, tears flowing. He asked her the question, and when she replied the man was astonished. His gloomy face quivered.

Had the servant gone mad?

Could she find only this name out of all the names in the whole world?

But he held his tongue and looked down. "Thank God you're safe," he murmured. Then he pointed to his wife. "Come here. We'll talk about this without any scandal."

Radiya looked daggers at Fayit Niddu, gave the cowering women a threatening glance, then went out behind her husband.

As they were walking to the 'umda's house, the scandal was leaving

Fayit Niddu's room to make its way around Hajar Narti, entering every house and reaching everyone. Sensible people hid in their homes, knowing that it would be madness to oppose Radiya's fury now. Some of the more impetuous went out and made for Fayit Niddu's room to find out how the scandal had originated.

Husband and wife walked glumly without speaking. As they went into their house, the slave and Bedouin girls who served them hid away to escape the storm. But Muhammad Said told them off, "Go out, all of you. I don't want anyone in the house."

They hurried out in alarm, seeking safety.

In almost eighteen years of marriage, Hajja Radiya had never known her husband to harbor so much anger. He ordered her to sit down, and she obeyed, while he walked around, giving vent to his anger and thinking.

She tried to speak to him but he gestured to her and she was silent.

More than once he sought refuge with God. Inside himself, he was looking for his old calm self. He was trying to repair the ground that had fallen from him, revealing anger and discontent.

When his heart had cooled again, he went back to his wife, sat down with her, and talked to her with his old voice and even temper.

"Hajja! Fayit Niddu is wrong, there's no question of that. But you're being blinded by your anger."

She shouted angrily, "The promiscuous servant is provoking me!"

His face grew dark at her fury, but he restrained himself and replied, "What's happened has happened. But people can't be saying that Radiya bint 'Ali al-Nayir is having a fight with a servant! It's not right for you or for us."

"So I should accept that she names her daughter after Shahinaz, my brother's daughter? Are you happy for me to accept this?"

He used tricks as he tried to soften her stance, trying as hard as he could to budge her. But the woman was like a mountain planted in the earth. After a little, they agreed that she would leave it to him to deal with it and that she wouldn't put her head near that of Fayit Niddu.

He sent for the slave girl and she came, trembling with fear. He spoke to her gently in front of his wife, who was smacking her lips so angrily that they bled. Then he took from her the birth certificate with the name Shahinaz on it and ripped it up.

Fayit Niddu's heart was also ripped apart as she saw the first of her dreams for her baby blown away as if they were nothing. Muhammad Said ordered her to go back to Dabba and get a new certificate in another name. He told her, "Choose a suitable name, Fayit Niddu. Call her 'Izz al-Qawm after your mother."

The slave-girl bowed her head and did not reply.

"I am making a suggestion, not ordering you. But don't repeat your mistake. There are lots of names; choose one you like."

He thought that if Fayit Niddu wanted to outwit his wife, she would call the girl Radiya next time. He almost laughed at this idea. But he quickly suppressed it and remained calm and silent.

The night before Fayit Niddu returned to El Dabba to change the name of her child, Sukaina bint al-Badri intervened, like a rainstorm pouring down during a drought.

Her sister-in-law pleaded with her and tried to placate her until eventually she became calmer. Then she asked for her permission to intervene. Radiya, feigning an anger that was no longer there, told her, "All this is because of your brother, 'Abd al-Hafez. He has done what he has done and we must put up with his nature."

Sukaina teased her and apologized. She reminded her, "Mistress of the village, ruin is in the nature of men. But what can we women do?"

Radiya smiled despite herself. "You are right. Men are tight shoes, but sore feet cannot be put up with!"

Sukaina gave a cheerful laugh, like the rustle of a breeze between the palm trees in the afternoon.

The following day, Sukaina bint al-Badri, the wife of Hajj Bashir, the brother of the district sheikh, son of the 'umda and grandson of the 'umda, traveled herself with Fayit Niddu, the broken slave, to the town of El Dabba, where they stayed at her sister's, Wazin al-Dahab. She called the child Abir after the daughter of 'Abd al-Rahman al-Badri, her brother, who was employed in the port at Port Sudan.

Who was like Sukaina bint al-Badri?

✸

"May God have mercy on her. She was an angel, by God. We never knew anyone like her and never will."

✸

As Shahinaz—the lady of the name—took to the dance floor, proudly watched by her aunt, Abir was leaving the surgery, hiding in the bosom of the night.

Ahmad Shigrib sent 'Abd al-Razeq home before his recovery was complete so that the surgery would be free for him. He caught Abir at Mahjoub's bus stop in the crowd of people welcoming the new arrivals. He waved to her and she escaped from the crowds and followed him.

As some boys bumped into her, they brushed against her and harassed her, but she passed on silent as a shadow.

When she had made herself naked for him Shigrib looked at her scraggy body. She was thin, with protruding bones, and her skin was dark, and a little rough. Why should she be so attractive?

"Are you a sorceress?" he asked her.

She shook her head to deny it.

"Why do you do this?"

She looked at him with her child-like eyes; a young girl of thirteen, naked in front of him, fresh as a palm frond.

She gave off a scent of arousal that was warm as embers on a winter's night.

He let out a deep breath. He didn't understand, and perhaps he wouldn't understand, but he didn't care.

He walked toward her, mounted her, and she bore him to the heavens.

✸

THE GHAJAR ARRIVED at no particular time and left in the same way.

They moved from place to place like a ball of straw carried by the wind. They left their lodging under the palms on the eve of the Prophet's Birthday. They went into the village and ate and drank and came to people's houses begging.

Most people chased them away and treated them harshly.

"How about working instead of begging?"

"God forgive our ancestor. It was him that left us the legacy of not working," the ghajar replied, men and women alike, in their thick, drawn-out voices.

No one knew, perhaps not even the ghajar themselves, who this ancestor was. But he was their constant reply to the question of why they refused to work or provide service. They simply used the argument of an old ancestor who had told them never to work and not to live in one place. These two commands were the sole inheritance of the ghajar. So they moved from place to place and begged. And they also stole, without the knowledge of the local people. They were not thieves but they were like birds, not believing that the farmer owned the ripe fruit. What they found, they took. And what they wanted, they begged for. Then they picked up an assortment of their things and went away.

On Friday morning, the locals saw them leaving in a long line. They were walking south on foot. Perhaps they would stop in Quraysh

Baba or perhaps they would just pass through. They would stop wherever the wind blew them.

They traveled, leaving behind both contempt and satisfaction, especially with the al-Badri family, on whose land the ghajar stayed whenever they came. They never swapped it for anything else. It was an old condition, by which this land had become the al-Badri family's land—a condition imposed by the old al-Nayir 'umda, in obedience to the order of his mother al-Afiya.

That was their reward for Bahiya's family the year they settled in Hajar Narti, though it is said she had died months before.

Al-Afiya was sad for the woman she had known for years. Her heart was weighed down by Bahiya's debt. So she determined to honor her family.

Her son, al-Nayir, was negotiating with one of the al-Badri family to sell him a piece of land. Al-Nayir raised what he was asking and al-Badri lowered what he was offering. When al-Badri was about to relent, al-Afiya intervened, and forced her son to accept a price lower than the one he had rejected at first. But the ground was only sold subject to a condition.

"It will be a campsite for the ghajar whenever they stay in Hajar Narti."

The al-Badri family grumbled at an unintelligible condition. "What have we got to do with the ghajar? Let them stay on your land or any old place!"

But al-Afiya emitted thunder and lightning.

She wanted to honor Bahiya's family, but she wasn't about to give the ghajar a permanent dwelling on her family's land. How could she know how this would develop in time?

The condition was extraordinary. Some of the al-Badri family found it demeaning. But they could not let pass the opportunity to buy land from the 'umda, al-Nayir.

If the condition for the ghajar to stay on the land was demeaning for them, the 'umda's sale of the land to them was demeaning for him.

Al-Afiya took advantage of that old resentment and fulfilled her wish. And so, she repaid her debt to Bahiya—a debt to whose existence no one can swear except for 'Izz al-Qawm's stories about her mother in her dotage.

The dubious story maintains that the bride al-Afiya was surprised by her husband Muhammad al-Hasan coming in to her room carrying a whip. Was it the third night when she had been waiting in her bridal dress, or was it later, after she had given up waiting? We won't know that, but we know that Muhammad al-Hasan beat his bride hard before she realized what was happening. She screamed and tried to run away, but he pursued her, seized her, and threw her on the ground. Then he put his foot on her chest and continued to beat her. His face was flushed with desire, as breath followed breath—as if he was swimming in the Nile, flirting with the current. Whenever she screamed, his eyes lit up. He beat her so hard her gown split open; so hard, he made her bleed. The whip left bloody stripes on her skin, on her back, belly, thighs, and legs.

When she was exhausted and had curled up inside herself like a worn-out rag, Muhammad al-Hasan took her.

She knew his "peg." He put his member, like the foot of a wooden bed, inside her. Everything the women had told her about men, but larger.

He was excited and out of control. He took her like a storm, and she wailed and climaxed under him, crying from fear, from surprise, from pain.

He covered her as powerfully as a camel mating with a she-camel. And she climaxed like a she-camel covered by a camel.

She knew the secret of her husband. The bloody lines on her body explained everything to her. She knew what aroused him and what made him desire a woman. She understood his previous failure, and she feared his next success. Would every night be like this?

When he got off her he left her unkempt and insulted, ripped apart by pain. Would this sick, thin, sixteen-year-old girl put up with this sort of love-making for the rest of her life?

She bore it for another night. Then another. Then a third night. But after less than a month she no longer had the patience to endure it. His wild nights had left scars on her body, and she was swollen like a water jar. She avoided inquisitive questions from the women, and showed patience until her patience ran out. Then she resisted him with all the determination she could muster. She grabbed his hand holding the whip and wrestled him for it. She bit his palm. But that aroused him even more. He slapped her and kicked her, laid her out on the floor, and put his foot on her face. He spat on her and brought the whip down on her chest. She screamed as if she were being sacrificed. And indeed, she was being sacrificed.

How weak her stratagems, how narrow the possible escape routes.

If she surrendered, he would beat her until he was aroused, and if she resisted, he would fight her until he was aroused.

She was a stranger to the village—so some of the accounts of her ancestry declared—so she had no support and no one with whom she could take refuge.

Should she run away from her husband and return to her family? If she did that, she would bear the disgrace so long as she was alive. But what torment would she suffer if she stayed!

Her search for a solution was what led her to Bahiya.

Fate brought Bahiya the ghajari to her threshold. She knocked at her door one summer's afternoon. She came to beg, as ghajar always do. The servant told her off but she insisted on her demands.

The mistress of the house, al-Afiya, saw the ghajari woman, who was older than her but a similar size—about twenty, perhaps, but slim and scraggy like her. Her skin was fair but covered in scabs and dark patches. Her eyes were green, like a cat's, and her voice was thick, drawn out, and expressionless.

Suddenly, al-Afiya had an idea. Despite her youth and lack of experience, she was a proud girl, too proud to seek a solution in the village, for she knew that her secret would not be kept by either slave or freewoman.

If she asked for help, she would find herself mired in scandal. If she turned to a servant she would obey her, but she would reveal her secret, and the whole of Hajar Narti would know what her husband liked and what he did to her.

But this ghajari, the migratory bird, the plant without roots, that was a different matter. This was a woman with no ties, who did not stay in one place, and who did not tell stories or gossip. Al-Afiya called her, and reluctantly the servants allowed her to enter. Then the woman took her to one side and made a bargain with her, for the ghajari to be her substitute.

'Izz al-Qawm's stories about her mother were like the stories of the old woman of Sab al-Zubairiya, more like fairy-tales that no one could be certain about. But they were the only accounts that were in circulation to throw any light on this incident. The only stories that explained the ties of friendship that had grown between al-Afiya, the mistress of the village, and the ghajari Bahiya.

Like all stories, and as is usual with stories, it wasn't important that they should be true; the important thing was that they should be amusing. And so they were.

Having heard it from her senile, illiterate mother, 'Izz al-Qawm put it about that al-Afiya met her husband Muhammad al-Hasan for the first time for months and discussed what he did to her.

"Your rights over me as a wife are something I am compelled to accept. But I can no longer bear it."

The man looked at her, pretending not to understand. He preferred not to discuss what he did, and thought his wife would not dare to discuss it either. She was an honorable girl from a good and honorable family. Girls like her didn't talk to their husbands about sex; only servants and slaves discussed such matters. A young woman from a good tribe wouldn't do that; she accepted what her husband did silently and bore his children.

"I can't bear that thing any longer. But I can't refuse you. So I've found a solution," she told him.

She told him what she had done and urged him to accept.

The man found her proposal strange. For a moment he was afraid of her. His wife was thinking and doing things that women in Hajar Narti didn't do! But he also liked and did things that men in Hajar Narti didn't do.

Perhaps they were right for one another.

"What about people?" he asked her.

"What people? The ghajar are silent as solid rocks. Our secret will be safe." (She deliberately said "our," to make him think they were together in the same boat. If he drowned, she drowned. If he was exposed, she was exposed.)

She held his hand and looked into his eyes. "I hope you will like it. We will be together. You can do whatever you like to her, everything you desire. Then afterwards I will be yours, at your command and subject to your wishes."

"And she? Will she accept?"

"She will be happy with it, in exchange for what I pay her. There is one problem!"

"What is that?"

"The ghajar come and go. They don't stay in one place."

"It is their ancestor's legacy to them, to be wanderers."

"Yes, which means you will have to be patient with them when they move away. We will wait together for them to return every few months. Can you be that patient?"

Could he manage it? He didn't know. But the whole idea excited him. It gripped him. And when men are aroused, they say "yes" to everything, to anything.

The following night, there were three people in the room. Muhammad al-Hasan, carrying his whip, al-Afiya in her bridal dress, her body bright with liniment, and Bahiya, with her coldness and her green eyes.

The start was confused. Muhammad al-Hasan was tense and nervous while al-Afiya was composed, directing everything decisively. She helped him beat the ghajari girl. More than once, she took the whip from him and beat her herself. She teased him as he kicked Bahiya hard. She told her off, ordering her to moan out loud, and forcing her to scream.

When Muhammad al-Hasan had finished he threw down his whip and leaped on his wife.

That was the most terrible thing he had known in his life. It was the most delicious thing he had tried in his life.

From that night on, for years afterward, Muhammad al-Hasan continued to share the two women. One revived him and inflamed him, and the other extinguished his desire and gave him pleasure when he reached orgasm.

❦

The whole village woke up late.

Those who had got drunk on Fayit Niddu's wine woke around noon. Those who had exhausted themselves singing and dancing woke after the sun had passed its peak. Those who had come from the capital in Mahjoub's bus were overcome by tiredness from the journey until the time for breaking their fast.

When they met, they exchanged smiles loaded with hidden meanings, as they recalled the previous night in a blur. But they knew that it had been a drunken evening, some people vomiting, others quarrelling without knowing it, some dancing lewdly, and others suddenly vanishing in pairs.

Wedding nights are nights of joy that know no bounds. So people like to recall them as "games." But when day breaks, everything returns to normal; caution goes back to its place and courtesies where they belong. But the stories go on, conveyed in secret by gossip.

Friday was the day of the Qur'an ceremony.

The drunkards had to wash their drunkenness from them; those who had dallied with women put their flirting behind them, and the teenagers cast off their sloth to be on time for the Friday prayer and Qur'an ceremony.

The women had to put off their licentious dancing, the remnants of their ululations, and the memories of those who had flirted with them to prepare the wedding feast for the guests after prayers.

With the first Friday call to prayer, life crept back into Hajar Narti, as if the previous night had never been. Nothing remained of it except for quiet gossip.

The men hurried to wash, and the women to the kitchens. Then the alleys were filled with white gowns and enormous turbans making their way to the mosque.

'Abd al-Razeq came, limping from his injury. Some people teased him about what had happened to him "behind the water jars." He grimaced, not welcoming their jokes. He tried hard not to rest on his wound when he sat, and his face screwed up as he moaned to himself.

The mosque was packed with locals, people from the capital, and those from neighboring villages. Quiet whispers filled the place with a buzz, like bees returning to the hive. There was an occasional cough from the chest of Hajj Bashir, whose condition was deteriorating every day.

When he had woken just before noon, he had belched so hard from Fayit Niddu's wine that he almost vomited. The headache was tearing apart his head, every sound like an explosion in his skull. He was irritated by the light, like a thousand suns beating on his eyes.

He recalled the previous night. His temper, their quarreling, and the political arguments. They had gotten so drunk, there seemed to be no one sober left in the world. They drank until the walls swayed and the stars' gossip became heavy. They had abandoned the imported wines to soak themselves in Fayit Niddu's booze, which was fiery as burning embers; it really was "Fayit Niddu Walker," as they called it. The khawaja's wines could not be compared with it.

Bashir asked forgiveness of his Lord, and washed quickly, without eating anything, then reluctantly dragged himself to the mosque, battling his lethargy. He was still coughing blood and decided to consult Ahmad Shigrib after the ceremony.

The question would do him no harm. He would continue taking butter and smearing his body with oil and trying whatever the medical assistant recommended.

The preacher mounted his pulpit, and from a duplicated piece of paper, read a sermon to those present that they had already heard on more than one Friday. If they had been more attentive, they would have memorized it by heart. But their minds wandered, hardly taking in what he was saying. He regained their attention only when he mentioned the Prophet's name, and the place resounded with an inattentive murmur, "May God bless him and grant him peace."

The mosque was cramped and the congregation spilled out into the yard outside under a cane awning. It had an incomplete minaret, awaiting more contributions from people living in the capital.

A May warmth brushed the congregation and their sweat flowed. They tore off their large turbans and wiped the sweat off, waving the turbans to capture a waft of the breeze.

As the sermon went on, some of them started to clear their throats. The preacher tried not to notice, but the muttering grew louder, and from his position above them, he could see the congregation shuffling in their places. He was forced to read quickly. He finished his sermon then led them in prayer with part of the sura "He Frowned and Turned Away" in the first rak'ah and the sura "The Afternoon" in the second rak'ah.

When he concluded the prayer, the congregation sighed without embarrassment.

The preacher's face fell and he turned to them as if to criticize them. But their eyes were fixed on the registrar, who got up from his place, carrying his bag to the front of the mosque. Hajj Hussein al-Badri and the father of the bride followed him. Those sitting in the front row moved to form a circle around them, and the registrar read the wedding address, reminding them that God had permitted marriage and forbidden fornication, and had created them as peoples and tribes to become acquainted with each other. The two fathers joined their hands and repeated the wedding contract formula after the registrar.

When they had finished, he raised their hands and called, "The *fatiha*."

Everyone raised their hands and recited the *fatiha*, or at least pretended to. Then he wiped his hands over his face and shouted, "Congratulations!"

The congregation stood up. They were tetchy from their sleepiness, the cramped surroundings, and the heat. Voices of congratulation crowded with them around the place.

"A thousand congratulations."

"May you have health and sons."

"A blessed and fortunate marriage, God willing."

"Wishing you children soon!"

Many people made jokes, wishing marriage for each other.

Hajj Bashir felt burning knives cutting his chest in half. He could no longer control his cough. His chest was split in two and his sleeve was full of blood. He fled to the mosque door before anyone could see him.

The congregation would recall hearing the sound of his loud cough behind them as they were busy with their congratulations, when they suddenly heard a muffled knocking sound, and the coughing stopped.

Hajj Bashir was only a few steps away from the mosque door when the world went cloudy in his eyes.

He saw darkness hurtling in his direction.

Suddenly all the voices fell silent and he lost consciousness. As he staggered, he stretched out his hand, trying to grab hold of anything. But all he could grasp was emptiness.

The world was extinguished.

Hajj Bashir curled up on the ground with the sound of a muffled collision.

"The fire in my heart has been set ablaze by Sukaina."

Desire was tearing his heart to pieces, eating him alive.

Love had struck Bashir's heart as a youth. He had grown up with love for Sukaina inside him. When he looked back, he couldn't recall a day when she was not there in his heart. Since he was a child and she was a young girl. Ever since he likened her to a piece of wrapped chocolate, he had grown up with the fire of her love blazing inside him. It never died down, like a fire of canes.

He carried on giving her sugar stolen from their house store, empty bottles of Bint al-Sudan perfume, and bundles of firewood. The breeze betrayed the love between them, so they made a pact. But fate preempted it.

He was twenty years old and wondering about the best way to mention the matter to his father. How could the son of the 'umda Said al-Nayir ask to marry someone from the al-Badri family?

Relations between the two families had been bad for some time, but no one remembered when the rivalry had begun. No one knew the reason for the rivalry either. Genealogists in Hajar Narti traced the two families to a common ancestor hundreds of years ago. An Arab emigrant settled in Nubia. Possibly, he had come at the time of the feverish quest for gold in the Sudan. At that time, whole Arab tribes were on the move, shifting their tent pegs from the traditional Arab lands to plant them in Nubia. The emigrant had four sons and three daughters. They say that the al-Badri family and the al-Nayir family are descended from the third son. But there was bad blood between them.

They were rivals and competitors for centuries, in ancestry, deeds, and wealth.

And he, the young Bashir, would perhaps succeed his father as 'umda, now that education had taken away his brother Muhammad, who dreamed of being a poet in the capital.

Could the 'umda be from the al-Nayir family and his wife from the al-Badri family?

Would his family accept that? Would his father agree to ask for the daughter of Hussein al-Badri for his son? Would the al-Badri family accept it? Would Hussein al-Badri accept the idea of giving his daughter to the al-Nayir family?

His nightmare was that his father would accept but that the al-Badri family would refuse, wishing to boast that the 'umda, Said al-Nayir, had come to them as a suitor but they had rejected him.

If that happened, it would be a disgrace that would last as long as the palm trees stood in the groves of Hajar Narti.

If that happened, it would be a disgrace he would not be able to live with.

He was paralyzed by fear and nervousness.

While he was hesitating in the darkness Babaker Sati came and flew off with his girl, sweeping down from nothingness and carrying her off.

Babaker Sati's lineage went back to the nearby town of El Ghaba. It had no connection with Hajar Narti except an unconfirmed link in antiquity with al-'Afiya, the legendary ancestress of the al-Nayir family. Some stories said that Babaker Sati was descended from a sister of al-Afiya's, whose name no one in Hajar Narti could remember. This story depended on a previous claim that al-Afiya's origin lay in the village of Sab al-Zubairiya. It was said that her family was among the few to escape from the village disaster. Then marriage took al-Afiya to

Hajar Narti and took her sister to El Ghaba.

This unconfirmed connection with Hajar Narti, despite being connected with the al-Nayir family, was what led some women of Babaker Sati's family to propose Sukaina bint al-Badri (whose beauty was well known in the land) as a wife for him.

Babaker Sati was no less well known than she was. He was an officer in the Sudan Defense Force. The only officer in the whole region from the borders of the district of Dongola in the north to the Shayiqiyya territory in the south.

His name attracted pride and reverence among people. Indeed, some people swore by his head as if he were one of the Warariq sheikhs. Mothers would tease their children and joke that they wanted them to grow up to be like him.

He was a brave fighting officer in the Shendi infantry division of the Sudan Defense Force, formed in the mid-twenties after the Egyptian army had left. It was headed by capable British officers with the rank of *miralay*, under them were British officers with the rank of *onbaşı* (corporal), and directly under them were Sudanese officers like Babaker Sati.

The force, which had been formed about twelve years prior, had never entered a war or been tried in battle, but had imposed governmental authority by suppressing small tribal rebellions and transient security disturbances. Despite that, its Sudanese members, especially the officers, enjoyed the respect and admiration of the people.

Babaker Sati stood high in this admiration as he sent his request to become engaged to Sukaina bint al-Badri.

The al-Badri family received the request to be joined in marriage with extreme happiness. This was a relationship only seldom bestowed by time. In the whole district there were many ordinary soldiers in the Sudan Defense Force but only one officer, and that was Babaker Sati. And he was knocking on their door as a suitor.

A potential relationship like that could not be rejected.

But Hussein al-Badri was not as enthusiastic as his family about the relationship.

Hussein al-Badri resisted the pressure from his brothers and his family.

Negotiators came to him every day. Some of them came to him and broached the subject directly while others visited him on the pretext of friendship, then mentioned the subject as if it didn't concern them.

The man didn't dare contradict his family openly, but he didn't give them an unequivocal agreement either, and maneuvered to the extent he was able to.

"The girl's still young."

"The girl's sixteen. They marry younger than that."

"The girl doesn't know him and he doesn't know her."

"Since when did wives know their husbands? Marriage is a pact between men. And Babaker is a man that any family would be proud to have as an in-law."

"Marrying an officer in the Sudan Defense Force would mean living far from her mother and moving from place to place."

"Do wives hold back their husbands to be close to their mothers? It's up to the wife to follow her husband wherever he goes. There isn't a house in Hajar Narti that hasn't got a wife from another village in it. Should we take other people's daughters and refuse our own?"

"Does the difference in age between them seem appropriate? The man is in his mid-thirties!"

"Does age shame a husband? Men that are middle-aged and older have married young girls since God created the world. Our master, the Prophet, married our lady Aisha when she was half the age of Sukaina!"

He tried all the arguments and all the tricks. Then he promised to think about it.

But no one would give him a sufficient chance to escape. His brothers showed anger at the reputation of the sweet girl. It annoyed them that people should sing the praises of her beauty. Some cousins attacked Mahjoub for having written her name on the back of the bus.

A decent family wouldn't be pleased at having their women mentioned by every Tom, Dick, or Harry. It wasn't right that fools and people without work should sing the praises of their girl's beauty.

The pressures on Hussein al-Badri mounted.

His family reminded him of what this relationship meant in relation to the al-Nayir family. The 'umda's family that hadn't got an officer among either its sons or its in-laws. In fact, some of them were soldiers in the Sudan Defense Force, which would make their prospective brother-in-law higher than them in terms of authority.

But this argument, which attracted all his family, was the least attractive to Hussein.

The man was open to living with all her family. He had friendships in the al-Nayir family, as well as companions with whom he exchanged gossip and held drinking parties. He wasn't interested in his family's rivalry with the 'umda's family. In the end, they all lived in Hajar Narti. "And in the end, we will all be buried in one cemetery," as he used to say.

But he could not describe this argument to his family as stupid. He couldn't openly diminish the importance of being superior to the al-Nayir family.

He thought that perhaps by agreeing with his family to this marriage he might buy a little of their approval. Then they would reduce their annoyance at him for his lack of enthusiasm for the continuing rivalry. Perhaps his agreement to the marriage would persuade them that he had paid what he owed to the family, so they wouldn't ask anything else from him so long as he lived. He would constantly put pressure on them by reminding them that it was he who brought them their important in-law Babaker Sati. This was a good deed that none of them would be able to deny, so long as they lived.

Hussein al-Badri's position softened a little as he figured that accepting the marriage would mean peace of mind for his life in the future. He wouldn't be marrying his daughter off to a weak or unimportant man, but to a high-ranking officer. Perhaps it wasn't so bad. It certainly wouldn't harm her. He would be marrying her to a good tribesman, with a good position.

He haggled with himself over the problem.

He relented a little. And his family pressed him harder.

He loved Sukaina. But he loved life more.

In the end, after weeks of to-ing and fro-ing, Hussein al-Badri surrendered to his desire for a quiet life. He announced his agreement to the marriage, on condition that Sukaina accepted. A condition that might as well have not existed.

For no girl could refuse a husband, unless she wanted rumors to be spread about her.

✿

The stories say that the first time Hajar Narti recognized Wazin al-Dahab's gifts as a singer was at the wedding of Sukaina bint al-Badri.

The wedding took place in the middle of 1937. Dahab's voice stood out among the girls of the village like one of David's pipes. Fresh and moist, like a fine morning.

The al-Badri family marshalled all their influence and connections to boast of that wedding.

Hajar Narti was spruced up as never before to receive the in-laws coming from the town of El Ghaba.

The village notables stood to greet the guests. Pride filled the al-Badri family and anger ate the al-Nayir family's walls. Dahab sang and all were happy.

The in-laws, men and women, arrived in a procession, with the venerable officer at their head. Bashir never knew regret like that day.

The hatred he felt was like a fire eating at the palms. He wished the earth would swallow up everyone, the whole of humanity, so that no one remained except him and Sukaina.

If an earthquake struck Hajar Narti, he and she would escape. He would take her and flee, and they would not look back. Why couldn't the sun drop from its orbit and consume the officer and his family, Hajar Narti, the country, and the whole world?

When the plates of broth were served, he swore it was his flesh in them, not the flesh of a lamb. The meat was his flesh and the gravy was his blood. And the diners were tearing at his heart with pleasure.

His brother Muhammad came back to the wedding guests.

He brought with him stories of the capital, the gossip of politics, and the trivial things of the world.

What did it mean to try to arrange a conference for the graduates of Gordon College? What was the point of the independence they were demanding? They were arguing about the sovereignty of the country after the government of Nahhas Pasha in Egypt had made a pact with the British. What was the point of all that when Sukaina was about to marry Babaker Sati?

Sayyid 'Abd al-Rahman Pasha al-Mahdi had traveled to London to seek clarification on the sovereignty of Sudan. He should have asked the British about Sukaina. He should have asked the king about love.

When the Egyptian army left thirteen years ago, a number of Sudanese conscripts had left with it. They had refused to abandon the service of the Khedive. So why shouldn't the British leave and take their Sudanese soldiers and Babaker Sati with them?

The Khatmiyya sect, to which his family belonged, supported Egyptian policy in the country. And the Ansar faction, to which Sukaina's family belonged, supported British policy in the country. The intellectuals were split between Sir Ali al-Mirghani and 'Abd al-Rahman Pasha al-Mahdi.

This nonsense was preoccupying his brother Muhammad so that he never spoke of anything else. And the notables listened to him, mesmerized. One of the elders said, "By God, the Egyptians are good people; Muslims and they pray like us!"

Muhammad, a young man who was passionate about politics of the capital, said, "The Egyptians were comrades in the struggle against British imperialism, but after the Treaty, they returned us to the Condominium Agreement of 1898. They betrayed us."

Another elder said, "The British created schools and projects for us. By God, their justice was better than Turkish or Egyptian rule."

"The British didn't do anything except create more divisions between us. They gave al-Mirghani the title of Sir and gave the land and government commissions to 'Abd al-Rahman ibn al-Mahdi."

The elders on both sides became annoyed, as each party shouted corrections.

"Sayyid 'Ali al-Mirghani! Don't say al-Mirghani like that! Aren't you afraid of being punished for disrespecting the descendant of God's Prophet?"

"Sayyid 'Abd al-Rahman! Don't say 'Abd al-Rahman ibn al-Mahdi! Don't you respect Sayyid ibn al-Imam al-Mahdi, on whom be peace?"

"School children—what do they fill their heads with?" said the 'umda Said al-Nayir. "They don't respect elders. What have graduates done for this country? Men like Sayyid 'Ali al-Mirghani and his deputies are the people who serve Sudan."

One of the al-Badri family corrected him, "And men like Sayyid 'Abd al-Rahman!"

Muhammad protested, "Everyone signed the book of loyalty to Britain. They all traveled to offer their loyalty to the British king."

Looks turned to the important officer, the elegant brother-in-law. The officer smiled but did not venture an opinion.

Bashir wanted the officer to give his view. He was a soldier in the Sudan Defense Force, so he doubtless supported the British. He worked under their authority. Perhaps he would say something to anger his new in-laws. Then the tragedy would end before it began. But Babaker Sati spoke judiciously, "What do children and school kids understand about the country and politics?"

Everyone laughed and shared his scorn. Muhammad al-Nayir cringed, and Bashir's heart was on fire.

The ignorant conversations about politics ended safely and did not spoil the wedding. They exchanged jokes and stories, as if they were not at odds.

Bashir was ready to stand and applaud Farouk, King of Egypt, Ruler of Nubia, Kordofan, and Dar Fur, or George VI, King of Great Britain and Ireland—anything to make the marriage successful. He would swear allegiance to Ibn al-Mahdi, or take the oath of allegiance to al-Mirghani, it didn't matter. He would do anything now so that those present would argue and the Qur'an ceremony would be canceled.

Don't recite the fatiha, *the bridegroom is an officer in the British army, people.*

They recite the *fatiha* and don't care.

Don't complete the contract, the country is divided between loyalty to Egypt and loyalty to Britain.

They complete the contract and don't care.

Don't ululate, Sukaina is mine. I promised her turtledoves.

The women ululate and take no notice.

Happy with the connection and the marriage, enthusiasm carried Hussein al-Badri away as he announced that he was giving a feddan of land to his daughter Sukaina. His enthusiasm inspired his uncles on both sides of the family and they shared his generosity. After the afternoon prayer, Sukaina became the wife of the officer Babaker Sati and owner of no less than fourteen feddans of the al-Badri family's best land.

In front of his eyes, murky with tears, Babaker Sati, the important officer in the Sudan Defense Force, took away his beloved. The village sent them off, saying farewell to them as the bridegroom and his wife made their way to the town of El Ghaba.

He took her away, leaving Bashir al-Nayir with his grief and a broken heart.

He took her away, and Sukaina bint al-Badri was no longer the prettiest girl in Hajar Narti.

She had gone.

※

A woman asked him: "Did you like her, Bashir?"

He craned his neck to look closer then said, "Sweet as a piece of wrapped chocolate!"

※

Let my heart go and leave me a little life.

Bashir tried to forget his beloved who had become the wife of another man.

He tried to snatch her from him, but his flesh was torn, and she became more firmly embedded in him.

How do lovers find consolation?

How do lovers sleep?

His night was a series of hallucinations, filled with her face and her smile; his day a string of memories of her eyes and her head, which inclined to the left when she was speaking.

The days passed and the passion did not let up.

The days passed and his wound would not heal.

Events happened but nothing could distract him from his passion. Then his father, the 'umda, Said al-Nayir, suddenly died.

He was standing, settling accounts with his farmers when without warning his eyes stared, his speech became heavy, and he started to sway.

He collapsed like a tall palm tree blasted by the wind.

He gave a snort, and died in the arms of the people carrying him before they could bring him to his house.

The tragedy shattered Bashir. *His lover had been gone a year and today his father had died. What a life this was, what a world!*

His uncles supported him to hold him together but he was inconsolable, like a woman who has lost her child. They spoke to him of shame, manhood, and patience in disaster, but he answered them with the tears of a crazed mourner.

The al-Badri family emerged from its isolation to demand the office of 'umda. The al-Nayir family stopped supporting Bashir and sent for his brother, the student in the capital.

"Come at once! The British will give the office of 'umda to al-Badri. You must come urgently to inherit your rights."

Muhammad Said al-Nayir came to take up his family's inheritance. He left the capital, politics, and poetry, took on the trust and became 'umda. He left behind the efendis who were expecting him. But he continued to subscribe to the *Hadarat Sudan* newspaper from the capital and the *al-Risala* and *al-Hilal* magazines from Cairo.

Muhammad surrendered his position as an efendi, but Bashir did not surrender his love.

He was pursued by grief. He walked like an empty skeleton, a lifeless image.

His brother gave him some advice. He portrayed marriage as a good thing in his eyes. But al-Bashir neither heeded nor heard.

He died a double death.

But time had something in store for him.

Amusing stories always have something in store.

And Bashir's story was like that.

The world was turned upside down by war. The whole world was loud with it, everything battered by madness. But as the British waged war, backed by their colonies, news came from the capital.

The Italian army entered the town of Kassala in the east of the country in July 1940. The Sudan Defense Force withdrew from the town after a battle in which the British spoke in glowing terms of the valor of the Sudanese troops. But Kassala fell. The country reeled from the Italian invasion that started from the Ethiopian border. The road to Khartoum was open. Would it be the end of the British?

Bashir's heart clung to his hopes. The Italians would defeat the British, their army would leave the country, and Babaker Sati would go with them in defeat. But would the al-Badri family let their daughter go with the British armies? Her mother had been very upset and cried for long nights when Babaker Sati took her from El Ghaba to the town of Shendi where his army division was based. The mother complained and demanded that her daughter come back from Shendi. But her husband reproached her and told her to be sensible and keep quiet. Would she accept that Sukaina should go with the British armies to God knows where? Where would the defeated armies go? They could go to hell, on condition that Sukaina returned to Hajar Narti.

But the British were not heading for a defeat.

They mustered their forces and redoubled their endeavors.

The Sudan Defense Force advanced eastwards to meet the enemy. They were followed by alarm, but also the support of the people.

Unlimited support for the British. All the country was praying for a British victory. There were songs everywhere.

> *May they return home safe,*
> *May they return home safe, O God,*
> *May they come back safe and visit,*
> *O God!*
> *Let them come back*
> *With tanks and machine guns,*
> *O God,*
> *My thoughts were preoccupied*
> *And my tears poured down,*
> *The train has left.*
> *I wish I were a compartment in the carriages of that train,*
> *O God,*
> *The train has taken the beloved away*
> *How difficult is separation!*
> *She will not be here on the nights of joy.*
> *O God*
> *Let them come back*
> *Our officers, victorious,*
> *O God.*

An Italian plane bombed Khartoum, but it did not break the high spirits. Everyone was praying for the British and the Sudanese soldiers. Donations were collected—the length, breadth, and depths of the country, even in Hajar Narti.

The 'umda Muhammad Said al-Nayir himself presided over the collection of donations, traveling at the head of a delegation to present them to the government and assure them of their support and loyalty.

The country held its breath as it waited in anticipation.

There were battles in Kassala, Keren, and Asmara. The Defense Force advanced. Babaker Sati sent his wife to his family in El Ghaba as his unit was going east.

Savage fighting and a grinding war.

The British or the Italians?

Would the enemy be defeated or would Khartoum fall?

The country sincerely prayed that God would grant the British and their king victory over the Italians and Il Duce.

And Bashir prayed for himself and Sukaina.

Then…

As on the Night of Power…

All their prayers were answered.

News of the victory came joyfully, bearing a good omen for the wounded lover.

God bless the Italians' rifles.

※

Our trenches are dug
The year nineteen forty is the year of victory
We'll play ball with Il Duce
And here is the goal
Hey, dude, may God help me
For I must water the lemon tree

※

The heavens are generous to the man who prays.

In the land that looked as if it had been created by chance, quickly and with no clear plan, the heavens could answer at any moment.

In honor of the river that comes from paradise, the heavens sent their gifts to the drowned on the thirsty dry land, stuck in this country by reason of their birth. They did not choose to be here, they sprang up on the banks of the river of paradise. They did not bring the water but they drowned on its shore.

The heavens sometimes teased them and answered their prayers.

The British beat the Italians, and the Sudan Defense Force drove back the invaders.

At the end of March 1941, the Sudanese rapid forces entered the Eritrean town of Keren. Then they pursued the retreating Italian forces to the town of Asmara, which surrendered, exhausted, to the allied forces, at the head of which were Sudanese soldiers.

Joy spread throughout the land, which broke into joyful song:

> *God be with me*
> *I must water the lemon tree*
> *Hey, dude*
> *My God be help me*
> *Mussolini the Italian*
> *Hitler the German*
> *Your character is like that of the devil*
> *I don't give a damn about Russia,*
> *Iraq and Greece,*
> *Austria and the Balkans,*
> *China and Japan,*
> *Egypt and Sudan,*
> *All love Britain*
> *Hey, dude*
> *Oh, the trench that they dug*
> *Our guns that they charged*
> *The British were victorious*
> *They brought the flag and came*
> *From Asmara*
> *Hey, dude, may God help me*
> *For I must water the lemon tree*

Keren was a resounding victory. It satisfied the thirst of the people of the country for praise and pride. And in Keren, Babaker Sati fell, crowned with pride and deserving of eternity in praise.

The stories would become weightier as the years passed. Whenever Babaker was mentioned, his part in the battle would be exaggerated, until after some years he had become its only hero, its sole combatant, the man who conquered Keren, expelled the Italians from it, then fell, a victim of their stray bullets as they fled before him.

His town of El Ghaba would crown him as a mythical liberator and the rest of the region would take its stories from there. Hajar Narti would weave yet more, for the man belonged to it by virtue of his relations through marriage. The hero who single-handedly terrified the Italians so much that even Il Duce himself congratulated his defeated forces on killing the legendary knight. Rome saw in the fall of Babaker Sati compensation for the loss of its colonies in East Africa.

As for Bashir…

Bashir the lover…

The news hit him and drove him mad. It was morning in their house, the 'umda's old house before it was destroyed by the flood in 1946. He heard the wailing but took no notice. He stayed propping himself up there without caring. With dead eyes he followed his three-year-old brother Rashid as he ran in the courtyard as naughty children do. An orphan who did not know his fate. He had been born a few weeks after the death of his father. His mother called Bashir, to ask him about the noise and shouting, but he turned his face to the wall, pretending to be asleep, and did not answer her. His mother sent the servants and they brought her the news that al-Badri's house had a fatality in it. The women wailed and the men left quickly. Let the al-Badri family all perish, as a punishment for what they had done! Let them wail for a thousand thousand years until their hearts burned as his had done. He sat up from his reclining position and got up to leave the house, to escape the duty of presenting condolences and being polite to people he hated.

He went to the pen but found only an old horse worn out by the years. He untied him, seated himself on top of him and set out to the East, away from the houses, wandered until the sun began to set, then returned as he had no alternative.

He found the village calm, with no shouting or noise. Had they all died, leaving only him alive?

The servants greeted him with the news confirmed.

For a second, he froze. Had heaven really been generous to him?

"News has come from El Ghaba that Babaker Sati, the husband of Hussein al-Badri's daughter, died in the war."

They said it again.

They repeated it to my ears.

They shouted it.

They sang it.

Babaker Sati dead?

After four years, like a lifetime?

Babaker Sati had died?

Babaker Sati had died?

Babaker Sati had died?

He had died?

Had he gone to the place from where no one returns? Had the earth embraced him, never to release him till the Day of Resurrection?

He leaped down from the horse and prostrated himself before the astonished servants.

He rolled his face in the earth.

He thanked God as he had never done before.

He felt a faith that had never visited him before.

O God, praise and thanks to you for your blessings!

O God, praise and thanks to you for what you have decreed!

Let Babaker Sati go to the heights of paradise or stay forever in the pit of hell. It didn't matter. What mattered was that he was no longer here.

Let him die a hero or choke to death. It didn't matter. What mattered was that he was no longer a barrier between him and Sukaina.

"Where is everyone?" he asked, his face lit by joy like a full moon.

"Everyone's gone to El Ghaba to present condolences."

"Everyone was there. Sukaina was there. And Babaker was no longer here!"

Was…?

He jumped on his horse and worked him up to a run. The old horse ran as if he was Buraq. He ran without stopping. He passed through villages, and the people saw him and called out. But he didn't stop. He went along the shortest roads. He made his horse jump every hurdle. There was nothing today between him and Sukaina. No distance today could keep him from Sukaina.

He was seized by madness.

He couldn't hear or see.

He was seeking his dream, that was all.

He was hastening to Sukaina.

And his journey was a long one.

At evening prayer time, the horse knelt before the house of condolence in the town of El Ghaba. It snorted, demanding air. Then it collapsed on its face, as if it had run aground. Bashir fell off it. But he didn't care. He got up again, leaving the horse to die, and rushed into the ceremony.

In front of the eminent people of the district, leading residents of El Ghaba, the dead man's family, and the al-Badri and al-Nayir families, people of Hajar Narti and mourners from all the villages—El Kurd, al-Abiriyya, Karamkul. al-Konj, Quraysh Baba, Sab al- Zubeiriya, and Sarwa—he leaped in front of Hussein al-Badri and shouted as frantically as he could, "Hajj Hussein, I have come as a suitor for Sukaina, so that no one else can get there before me."

Everyone present was struck dumb.

And rumour put on its sandals, to run and announce what had happened.

❧

God bless the Italians' rifles.

❧

Hajar Narti was in commotion because of what had happened.

The village was seething, harboring evil. The al-Badri family was overcome by anger at the scandal that had occurred in the presence of the whole district, while the al-Nayir family consumed itself over what Bashir had done, and made its pleasure known to its enemies. Between the two families, people circulated gossip and made alliances.

"By God, he's got no right to create a scandal like this in front of everyone! But that's the nature of the al-Nayir family. They despise everyone else!"

"We've never heard of what happened to you happening to a respectable family!"

"The al-Badri family has no one of any consequence except Bashir. I heard they decided to attack him. Keep calm!"

"We heard there was something between them before the wedding."

"Did the lad commit a crime by asking to marry their daughter? God, we should thank him! One of the best young men, and he wants to marry a widow of theirs who lost her husband when he died after four years!"

"You'll let the actions of the al-Nayir boy pass off like that with no punishment?"

"The al-Badri family are arrogant by nature and despise other people. What did your son do that they should stir the world up like this?"

"The al-Nayir women say that Sukaina is bad luck and they are not willing for their son to marry her!"

"The al-Badri girl bewitched him a long time ago before her marriage. That's what made him do what he did."

"Of course, I'm on your side, no doubt of that."

"The whole village is with you, except for those with vested interests."

Muhammad Said almost hit his brother, as he shouted at him, "You've made a scandal of us in front of everyone."

Then, to anyone who asked, he said, "A young man asks for a woman's hand from her father. Either they accept or they refuse. There's no need to say any more about it."

His uncles were of one mind. They shouldn't throw themselves on the mercy of the al-Badri family, who would forgive them if they wanted and punish them if they wanted. They would have to do something that would put the al-Nayir family in the right. But what could they do, when every village was a witness to what Bashir had done?

In the al-Badri family, the only topic of conversation was how to respond to the insult the al-Nayir son had directed towards them. Except for Hussein al-Badri.

Hussein was embarrassed about what the youth had done but he wasn't angry. He tried to gently calm his family. His brothers and in-laws were behind the madness at a distance.

One young man threatened to burn the al-Nayir family palms. Hussein gently responded, "My son, no one plays with fire! One match in the village will burn all of our palm trees. Fire does not select palm trees on the basis of certificates of ownership!"

The he added, filling out his advice to everyone, "The proverb says: 'If a man rips your coarse fabric, don't rip his silk.' That is, the sensible man doesn't take excessive vengeance. The punishment must be in proportion to the deed."

"Their action was black, but what they can expect from us will be even blacker than their deed."

"There's only one offender. Bashir made an error in asking for Sukaina as his wife on the day when she was accepting condolences for her husband. It's not right that his action should be linked to the whole of his family."

"He wouldn't have dared commit such a crime if he hadn't belonged to the al-Nayir family."

Madness stalked the village. Only God knew where things would end.

Hussein al-Badri secretly blamed Bashir. Not for what he had done on the day for condolences but for hiding his desire for Sukaina. If he had asked him for her before her marriage he would have agreed, even after Babaker Sati had become engaged to her. He had a hidden affection for the young man, as if he was his own son. And he respected his father, the late 'umda, Said. However much he hated his family, the al-Nayir family were cousins to the al-Badri family. They claimed descent from the same ancestor.

He observed his brothers' irritation and how people were spitting poison at the problem. He knew that if things weren't settled quickly things would happen that couldn't be undone.

He thought of a step to end all the problems and bring the crisis to an end.

But it was a step that demanded boldness. He was searching for it within himself, but it eluded him. How he wished he could take it!

Peace required a frightening leap in the dark. He would protect Hajj Hussein and visit the young 'umda, Muhammad Said al-Nayir, at night.

They talked for a long time.

The 'umda was afraid of his uncles. And Hussein al-Badri was afraid of his brothers. Both were afraid of discord.

They encouraged each other. They would take a leap in the dark.

They agreed. They sent for the young lover and he came. They gave him the good news.

When God decrees something, it is done.

❧

Time passed, as autumn clouds pass in the sky.

The months of the waiting period disappeared, and the dream grew closer.

Bashir al-Nayir would marry Sukaina al-Badri.

The dove's prophesy would come true. Love would triumph over the two families' enmity.

Hussein al-Badri plunged into his battle against his family. He persuaded them, with some difficulty, that the best solution to the scandal would be to accept the request of the young suitor. The 'umda, Muhammad Said al-Nayir, also plunged into his battle against his family. He persuaded them, with difficulty, that their best way out of the scandal would be to bury it with a wedding.

Bashir al-Nayir would marry Sukaina and people would forget his scandalous behavior. Hajar Narti wouldn't blame a man for marrying a woman he wanted.

Bashir visited his new in-laws. He tried to show them respect and affection. A good word can take off the lion's moustache. Gradually, their attitude of anger changed. Just as a flower can change into a lemon under the eye of the beholder, so the angry rejection turned into an affectionate acceptance.

The lemon would ripen.

The angry quarrel between the two families turned into an expansive affection.

Bashir al-Nayir would marry Sukaina.

The two families would (temporarily) forget the quarrel between them. What was in the heart would remain there, but Sukaina was Bashir's.

The months of the waiting period grew fewer, and the dream drew nearer.

How beautiful life is when it smiles. How beautiful it is when it draws closer.

Sukaina, end of a dream

From your smile the world was created. And to your eyes the River Nile flows.

Bashir drowned in a happiness that turned him upside down.

Let the world rage as it willed; Sukaina was his, and after that nothing mattered.

❧

The year Bashir married Sukaina bint al-Badri, Su'ad was drowned.

Fayit Niddu raced the dawn every day.

Dawn never caught her sleeping. She would stir in the darkness before dawn, get her things ready, sterilize her cups, mix her cloves and cardamom and ginger, boil the coffee beans, then crush them in a wooden mortar until they became soft.

Abir woke to the pounding of the mortar.

She got up like a polluted autumn river, with wrinkled brow and swollen eyes, surrounded by sticky rust. She scratched her hair and leaned her back against the wall.

Her mother called her, "Don't be long. I don't know where you hide every day. But for once, at least, don't leave me alone to work!"

Abir nodded her head. Fayit Niddu gathered up her things, as she got ready to leave. "I'll call in at your uncle Bashir's on my way. I haven't seen him for two days. Have you visited him recently?"

Abir had seen him yesterday. She was sneaking out of Rashid's house and called in at Bashir's house so he could say he'd seen her and she could explain her absence to her mother.

"Yesterday."

"You didn't tell me. Visit him today. Don't leave them. They are your family. The 'umda Said's children are your uncles."

Abir got up, feeling sick. Her little chest felt swollen. She stretched, and looked at her mother without saying anything.

What would be her reaction if she knew what Abir did with one of her uncles?

Rashid could no longer do without her. Not a day went past without him lying in wait for her. He dragged her to his house, shut the pair of them inside, mounted her, then flew off. She came out to be met by Ahmad Shigrib, who dragged her to the surgery, shut the pair of them inside, embraced her then flew off.

Abir bore both of them to heaven, like a mythical horse that spread its wings and flew. She let them taste all sorts of pleasure, unheard of types of delight.

The skinny girl had been created from the nectar of passion.

She moved between the two lovers like a kiss from one set of lips to another. She carried delight and scattered it among them.

She urged Rashid to fulfil his promise through mediation and he promised to do it quickly. Shigrib urged her to let him marry her and she promised it quickly.

Shigrib became happier and gentler with the object of his desire. Abir made the world fairer in his eyes. He walked along the village paths, singing:

> *Even if just by a smile*
> *Say, I love you*
> *Just with a glance*
> *Even a passing one*
> *Say I love you*
> *If you dream in your sleep*
> *Say I love you*
> *If you send me your greeting*
> *Say I love you*
> *Every word from your lips*
> *Is a fair song*
> *Every glance from your eyes*
> *Brings consolation*

People looked at him and smiled. "The medical assistant is in love," they said.

He went into Fayit Niddu's shack and smiled at the people sitting there as if he had been missing them for months. They talked about anything and he laughed. They told him any old story and he was delighted.

They were talking about the late nationalist Ismail al-Azhari, who wore the calico suit and had died in a military prison four months ago. He died of disease and neglect.

"They say that al-Azhari, may God have mercy on him, was in a ministers' meeting, and one of the ministers was ill in hospital. When the meeting ended late, al-Azhari asked his ministers whether the hospital guard would let them go in after visiting hours."

They laughed, Ahmad Shigrib loudest of all.

"He was quite an exceptional man."

"May God have mercy on him. A thoroughly decent man."

"I saw his picture as he was raising the flag of independence in 1956 with al-Mahjoub. A civilized man and a fresh start."

"The world has no security."

Someone frowned and hummed:

Today we raise our flag of freedom
And history writes the birth of our nation.

Gradually, the merriment died down. They turned to the happy man. "How is Hajj Bashir?" someone asked.

Shigrib sipped his coffee. "Well, thank God!"

His curt reply did not satisfy their curiosity, and someone else repeated the question. Shigrib replied again, "Well, please God."

They tried to extract information from him but he was tight-lipped. He was reluctant to tell them anything to satisfy their curiosity.

"I visited him yesterday before coming here. May our Lord relieve his suffering," said Fayit Niddu.

But they didn't want Fayit Niddu's answer. They pursued Shigrib. He tried to escape their persistence by suggesting other subjects. He led them East but they insistently brought him back to the West. When he asked about the village's past history and its gossip, they answered quickly, without detail, to return to their original question.

After a lengthy game of cat-and-mouse, he was exhausted by their siege and surrendered.

"It is in God's hands."

Some weeks had gone by since Hajj Bashir came back from Dongola hospital. The doctors had confirmed that he had TB—"the evil disease," as people called it. There was nothing they could do now. The man had reached the final stages of the disease. There was no effective cure for it. He had returned to Hajar Narti, bringing his despair with him.

He was awaiting his end.

Shigrib said, "May our Lord give him a good end."

❦

Nur al-Sham ran from the kitchen to the room where Hajj Bashir was isolated. She called to the servants, slave girls, and Bedouin girls.

Her husband was coughing hard, then spitting and moaning. He was growing thinner every day. He had become dry as a dry branch, so thin that his eyeballs were almost falling out of his face. He was fighting the "evil disease" without hope.

She secured the blanket around him to protect him from the biting December cold. Seven months had passed since he collapsed in the village mosque. That was the day she became alarmed, as she still was.

She went in with him to the medical examination and treatment room in the hospital. She spent weeks beside his bed in Dongola hospital. Then she came back with him to the village to wait to be widowed.

She had lived by his side for nine years as a good wife. She had never disobeyed him or made him angry. Two years ago, she had given him his only son, Azhari.

She had been a child of seven when he married her aunt, Sukaina. She used to call him "Uncle Bashir." Then, before he married her, two years after the death of her aunt, she began calling him "Hajj."

Her uncle became her husband. But she continued to respect and honor him as she had done during her aunt's life.

She knew he didn't want her, and her grandfather, Hussein al-Badri, did not pursue Bashir to offer her to him in marriage to save her from the spinsterhood that she was approaching at the age of twenty-five—but for a different reason. She was a substitute for her deceased aunt and a sop to his demands for his rights to the inheritance of his late wife. Sukaina owned at least fourteen feddans of the best land in Hajar Narti and had inherited from her husband Babaker Sati a quarter of the agricultural lands he left in the town of El Ghaba and shops in the capital. Hajj Bashir easily got his share of her inheritance from Babaker Sati, but the al-Badri family was uneasy about his accepting Sukaina's inheritance of their land. It was difficult for them to see their land going to the al-Nayir family. Hajj Bashir continued to pursue them for two years. But he refused—out of respect for Sukaina's memory—to take the matter to court. After a two-year delay, Hussein al-Badri proposed to Hajj Bashir that he should marry his granddaughter, Nur al-Sham, but the proposal didn't find favor with Hajj Bashir and he made his excuses. But her grandfather wasn't content. He knew that this marriage would satisfy his family a little in regards to the future of his inheritance from them. Hajj Bashir was sixteen years older than her, so her grandfather expected that she would inherit everything back from him.

Nur al-Sham was a substitute for her dead aunt. And she was an important guarantee.

Hussein al-Badri argued with his family, "This is the best thing you can do!"

"To belittle us in front of the al-Nayir family! How can you pursue Bashir with an offer of your granddaughter?"

"The day Bashir al-Nayir dies, Nur al-Sham will inherit from him, and you will get back what you are after and more!"

"Can you guarantee that Nur al-Sham will not die in the same way Sukaina died, then the al-Nayir boy will demand a bigger inheritance from us?"

What they were saying hurt his feelings. They had stepped on the innermost part of his heart. Hajj Hussein al-Badri was not happy with what he was doing. But he regarded himself as compelled to calm the fears of his family and guarantee Hajj Bashir his share of the inheritance.

"Bashir legally has a right to half the property of the deceased, that is, he will inherit no less than seven feddans. Of what is left, her mother will inherit a sixth, about two feddans and a few shares. The rest is mine. The only thing upsetting you is seven feddans. If Nur al-Sham inherits them, then a quarter of these feddans, that is, about two feddans less a few bits, would return to you. We would only lose five feddans, which is nothing in exchange for your inheriting what the 'umda Said al-Nayir left to him. Those lands are limitless. So what do you want?

"And if he inherits from Nur al-Sham?"

"Are you praying for my granddaughter to die like my daughter?"

"I didn't mean that, Hajj, I just asked…"

"You didn't intend to, but you did."

Hajj Hussein al-Badri used his pretended anger to avoid blaming himself.

The woman Fatima, mother of the girl Su'ad, had been chasing the corpse of her daughter for about twenty years, while he was maneuvering over his daughter's inheritance just two years after her death. Why was his grief not like Fatima's grief? Was women's sorrow for their children greater and more sincere than men's sorrow? Did Fatima love Su'ad more than he loved Sukaina?

She was the apple of his eye and his heart's fragrance. How was it that he had thought so little of her death that he had started to discuss the legal niceties of inheritance?

His heart swung back and forth with grief. His tears flowed inside him as he tugged at his stick and argued in front of the people.

"Forgive me, Sukaina. Forgive me, my daughter!"

❧

Sukaina had lived for nineteen years as wife to Bashir al-Nayir.

Nineteen years in which he had tasted bliss and known the essence of happiness. What is the world without life in the shade of the beloved?

As he coughed on his bed, he was assailed by hallucinations. He moaned in his weakness but he heard Sukaina's voice. She was singing in a whisper,

> *Oh my beloved*
> *I am crazy for you*
> *From the day I fell in love with your beauty*
> *The armies of your love have worn me out*
> *The more you dally with me*
> *The more wiles I use against you*
> *O green one, the color of lemon*
> *You have taken away from me my sight*
> *And blinded my eyes*

It was her favorite song by Aysha al-Falatiyya. She would sing it as she filled the house with her shining presence. She would sing it as she filled his life with her joyful presence.

He felt her hand, the one that he loved, on his brow. He loved her small hand, with its full fingers. He remembered the four lines on her palm, their beginnings and their curves. How often had he passed his lips over these lines.

He had been possessed by desire until his mind dissolved. That was what angered Radiya. She despised his passion and the way he laid his heart at Sukaina's feet.

"We have lived to see a man from the al-Nayir family brought down by passion!"

Radiya created a battle of dust with Sukaina. Perhaps it was the jealousy of ancestors. Perhaps it was her anger at forming a marriage alliance with the al-Badri family.

Radiya criticized Sukaina's cheeks, which were smooth and had no tribal markings.

"Facial scars are our custom and our heritage. Ever since God created the world, our men and women have been scarring their cheeks with these tribal marks."

Her husband, the 'umda, Muhammd Said, tried to deflect her from her battle.

"What have people's cheeks to do with us, Radiya? Leave the woman to her husband!"

"What have we to do with a woman who lives among us and has become one of us? Her mother was ignorant of our customs, so should we be quiet?"

"Radiya, she is a wife who is in her mid-twenties. She will become a mother at any moment. What is the use of this? If she has a child, I promise I will only leave Bashir alone after he has put the marks on the cheeks of his children. But what can we do about a mature woman?"

"There is no one too grand for our heritage. Even the nomads put marks on their cheeks. The marks are a source of pride, as well as a decoration."

"A decoration that the woman dispensed with. So what can we do?"

"What sort of 'umda are you that you do not defend the heritage and customs of your people? Aren't you angered by children born out of wedlock by the slave girls? Doesn't it bother you that people are abandoning the tribal marks? Tomorrow perhaps people will give up girls' virginity and you won't interfere."

"There is no power or might except in God! Is the 'umda pursuing girls' vaginas as well?"

Radiya could keep neither still nor silent. She pursued her sister-in-law, trying to measure her smooth cheeks.

Bashir was overcome by shyness and didn't know how to defend his wife. He didn't dare clash with his sister-in-law and he pitied his brother's weakness before her. Whenever she pursued him, he fled.

"Your wife is no longer a child. She's not a baby now, to say to, 'Oh, look how sweet!' Aren't you embarrassed by her cheeks that are smooth as a baby's?"

How could he tell her that he liked his wife's cheeks smooth, with no tribal marks?

Sukaina the angel was not pleased by Radiya's anger. She was only three years older than her but she revered her like a mother. She accorded her the status as wife of the 'umda and mistress of the village. She hurried to her when Hajar Narti was full of rumors of Radiya's anger. She didn't consult her husband or delay.

"You are the crown on the head of every woman in Hajar Narti, Radiya. Death would be more bearable in my eyes than your anger."

"Just words! You speak well but play around with poor Bashir. Don't deceive yourself that I'm like him, Bint al-Badri!"

"I swear by the sheikhs of Warariq that I only say what I mean!"

Radiya searched in his face for a trick but could only find innocence there. His eyes were clouds of sincerity raining down love.

She snarled a warning, "Don't use words to play with me, Bint al-Badri! By the life of the Prophet of God, father of Fatima, I will not be deceived by you!"

"By the life of my Lord, the Prophet of God, I am not deceiving you and I will not return anything to you!"

"Vileness cannot deceive me."

Sukaina agreed to be bled out of respect for her sister-in-law. Radiya insisted, thinking that the woman was trying to trick her. They summoned 'Izz al-Qawm and she came, quivering with fat, weighed down by old age. Sukaina asked her to take the razor and make straight tribal marks on her cheeks, as was the custom of her tribe.

In front of Radiya's amazed glances, the old woman's trembling hand moved the razor along Sukaina's cheek. The blood flowed and the woman closed her eyes, silently biting her lips. 'Izz al-Qawm dressed the wounds with a piece of linen dipped in cumin and coffee beans.

Sukaina opened her eyes, blood covering her face. Linen and coffee grounds oozed from her wounds. She looked at Radiya, and said in a tearful voice, "Are you happy with this, O best of women?"

The locks on Radiya's heart were broken, its bolts and bars smashed. Sukaina had raided it as no other human being had done before. And Radiya herself was as astonished as she was, as she found herself lying in Sukaina's bosom, embracing her and crying, "Pardon, God and the Prophet, O best of daughters! Pardon, God and the Prophet!"

No one could any longer take Sukaina's place in Radiya's heart. The tight-lipped woman had fallen in love with her sister-in-law and loved her passionately.

From that day on, no one dared oppose Sukaina. Anyone that did so would be eaten alive by Radiya.

As for Bashir, he discovered that he liked his wife's cheeks scarred with the tribal marks. He loved her and loved everything about her. If anything changed, he would love what had changed.

He didn't love her because of what she was, he loved the way she was because that was how she was.

He licked her cheek and passed his lips over its furrows. And Sukaina gave him contentment such as no man had ever known before.

He was mad for her. He had turned into a dervish, sunk in the depth of the Prophetic presence. He wandered lost in her love, repeating, "Alive! Alive! Alive! Sukaina! Sukaina! Sukaina!"

If he left the house, he came back quickly. He only ate what she made for him. If he was delayed on business outside the village, he would return by night either riding or on foot, in cold, rain, or the heat of summer. He would not stay anywhere except at home.

His brother, Muhammad Said, laughed and said, "Passion humiliates the necks of men!"

He had years of happiness and he completed them.

Then life turned sour and turned it back on him.

❦

Abir came back into Hajj Bashir's house.

Nur al-Sham welcomed her. Abir bore her cousin's name. She loved her for her name, and for her deceased aunt's love for her and her mother. And she was also—though this is not something that was said openly—her uncle 'Abd al-Hafez's daughter. Abir called the slave girls, but Nur al-Sham sent them away from her, and took the girl to see her uncle Bashir.

He was hidden away in a dark, poorly ventilated room. It was warm, insulated from the cold weather outside. Abir could not see him clearly. A strange object in the dark room under a heavy cover. The sound of his breathing filled the place. The room smelled like the stomach of someone selling onions that had rotted for a long time.

She called Nur al-Sham.

"Abir, Fayit Niddu's daughter, is here, and sends you greetings, Hajj!"

Hajj Bashir snored and didn't move.

Abir's pent-up voice came out, "I hope you'll get better, uncle!"

The Hajj snored again and groaned, lost in his fantasies with Sukaina. He wasn't conscious of his surroundings.

She was raining in his heart now.

Sukaina passed like a cloud in his imagination, humming, "*When I wait for you to meet me, my rivals and enemies won't spare me...*"

He returned to a summer night when he was staying up with his brother. They were drinking and laughing together, he was happy, without a care in the world.

Then a frightened servant came to him. "Catch Sukaina!"

He sprung up, afraid.

It was a summer's night but he felt the cold coming over him.

He ran quickly and caught up with Sukaina.

It was a summer's night but he was shaking as he ran through the sand.

Nur al-Sham refastened the blanket around him when she saw him shaking.

She went out with Abir into the spacious courtyard and Abir asked her what she could do for her.

"Thank you, kind girl. The girls here can provide me with all the services I need."

She looked at her carefully. The young girl had a glow that a woman's eye could not mistake.

"Are you alright, Abir?"

She nodded her head.

"Is anything wrong? Are you in some trouble?"

She shook her head.

Abir offered to look after the baby, Azhari.

"He's asleep at his uncle's house. Hajja Radiya will bring him."

If Radiya was coming, Abir would have to leave. She didn't want to be seen by the old woman's prying eyes. She didn't want a clash with the old woman, who hated her as if she was made of devil's pus. Radiya despised her and insulted her as much as she could. She found pleasure in destroying her. Her mother, Fayit Niddu, tried to give her strength.

"Don't be bothered by what she says. She's an old woman, the wife of your uncle. Respect her and obey her."

But the old woman rejected Abir, even when she was obedient.

More than a year and a half before, Radiya had invited her to a gathering of her friends, with no warning and no particular excuse. She had simply invited her to make fun of her. After standing Abir up in front of her, she asked, "Do you know who your father is?"

She was a child of eleven. But she knew what the village was whispering about.

"You do know that you're a bastard, don't you?"

The women laughed.

"You know that bastards don't go to heaven? Have you learned that at school? Or do they teach you bad manners and nonsense at school?"

Abir fidgeted where she stood but did not reply.

"You're a bastard, and your mother has no morals. We'll marry you off quickly so that you don't create a scandal for us like your mother did."

Why were the women laughing?

What did I do that they should hate me like this?

Abir continued to hold her tongue, bowing her head down in silence. But the old woman didn't stop there.

The stories in Hajar Narti about that day would describe Abir's long patience.

Some women would privately say, for fear that Hajja Radiya would hear them, "The girl was polite. But the Hajja had no mercy on her."

What Radiya did had no reason. She was playing, that is all. She was teasing Abir and making her companions laugh, when suddenly the girl lifted her head.

She directed her glance deep into the eyes of the old woman, and in a challenging voice, said, "I'm the first in my class at school. And I'm going to be a doctor."

Radiya laughed, followed by the others. But Abir repeated her plan. "One day I will travel to university and become a doctor. And when you become ill, I won't treat you, I'll leave you to die."

The women were struck dumb, and Hajja Radiya was astonished.

"I'll leave you to die because you are a horrid woman who doesn't deserve to live. People will thank me. They'll say 'Thank you, Doctor Abir, for leaving that horrid old woman to die.'"

Radiya was frightened. "Would you pray against me, you bastard?" she shouted.

Abir fell silent once more but she did not bow her head again. Her eyes were filled with defiance, and the old woman cursed her.

That was the day Hajja Radiya decided not to send Abir to school again.

Fayit Niddu implored her. Abir apologized, with a stony face and a voice with no trace of regret in it, but the old woman stuck by her decision.

Abir would only go back to school over her dead body.

Fayit Niddu asked the elders to have compassion. But they evaded her, wondering about the value of school for a girl born of slaves.

"Do you really hope your daughter will become a doctor?" Muhammad Said asked her.

The young girl had not taken the name Shahinaz, and she would not become a doctor.

Sukaina was not ill. She was as bright as the sun.

She was laughing, and her mirth spread through the house as she helped the slaves and Bedouin servants to prepare supper. Her husband was spending the evening with his brother Muhammad Said but he would come back for supper. He only ate with her.

She was saying something when she cried out, clutched her right side, and her face suddenly turned moist with sweat. She staggered, and her servants caught her before she fell.

As she suddenly turned pale, a female servant ran to fetch Hajj Bashir.

Sukaina sank into oblivion with no warning. As Hajj Bashir came to the last sand dune near the house, he heard women shouting. He stood rooted to the spot as Sukaina suddenly expired. He had become alone, as he was created, and the world went back to darkness.

He was late that day in coming back. He went in and did not find her sweet spirit hovering there. He didn't hear her last words.

He called her but she did not reply.

He embraced her but she did not respond.

People crowded around him. *Where had they come from? When were they born?*

"Seek God's mercy, Hajj Bashir!"

"It is God's command, Hajj!"

"Remember God!"

He wrapped his turban around his waist and rolled in the dust.

Hajar Narti wailed. Indeed, the wailing can still be heard today.

The face of the village became ashen. Bashir lived to reject it and see it as a stranger.

Everything without Sukaina was nothing.

He saw her now in his hallucinations, shining as she walked.

"Why did you leave me, Sukaina?"

"I never ever left you, my darling."

"After you, it was a lifetime that could not be counted."

"I was waiting for you."

"Was I late for you?"

"For every meeting there is an appointed time."

"Has our time come?"

"Now, if you wish."

He stretched his hand out toward her.

"Take me."

"Do you know where to?"

"To where dreams slumber. To you."

He slipped his hand into the hand of the one he loved. He remembered the four lines of this palm. Their beginnings and their bends. How often had he passed his lips over these lines.

He would follow her to the light.

He would disappear there.

Forever... beside Sukaina.

THE NEWS WASHED through Hajar Narti like water seeping through a wall.

Rumor carried the news along, and it spread as people chatted. Winter departed, and summer raised its head in anticipation. People became absorbed in the news and smiled.

"Hajja Radiya will slaughter you," Fayit Niddu wailed.

She struck her cheeks and screamed but Abir was silent and unmoved.

"You have disgraced us! You have disgraced us! You have disgraced us!"

There was no longer any possibility of a cover up. Abir's belly had swollen and exposed everything.

The young girl was pregnant!

The news spread at a run between the houses, and the palm trees gossiped.

Despite Fayit Niddu's outburst, it was not so much a scandal as a source of amusement to people as they tried to work out the name of the father.

"Muhammad al-Siddiq."

"Muddathir Nureen."

"Ahmad Shigrib."

"Mu'awiya, Sayyid Ahmad Jabrallah's son."

"Al-Tahir Ibrahim."

"Mutawakkil."

'Uthman, Nafisa's son."

"Muhammad Ibrahim al-Badri."

"Al-Sadiq 'Umar."

"The son of the jeweler from Quraysh Baba, what's his name? Saad."

"Khalifa 'Abd al-Karim."

The list was a long one, with many names. Hajar Narti brought out its stories about Abir, and everyone shared them. Anyone who knew or suspected something told it, and those that didn't made something up.

"I caught her once with Murtada, al-Baqir's son, in the house of the old 'umda."

"I saw her going into the surgery after dark on her own and disappearing for a while."

"Very forward, she was. Ask me. I saw her with the boys behind the mosque."

The stories, true and false, spread among the people, mingling together as they pursued Fayit Niddu.

"I was ready to die for you to become a doctor. I was waiting for you to raise my head and take me from this village. What have you done to yourself and to me, my daughter, fruit of my womb?"

Abir pretended not to hear her.

"We are on our own. We have no one. Don't let temples and turbans delude you! We are on our own. We have no family, wealth, or respect. All the women who embrace me harbor contempt for me. It is not only Radiya who despises me. We are descendants from nowhere in a village that prides itself on its ancestry. No one respects us except when they need us, and we show them manners and obedience. You're not from the al-Badri or al-Nayir family, and your father isn't a landowner. You're Fayit Niddu's daughter. You only have me and I only have you. Why do you think your uncle 'Abd al-Tamm fled this village? He escaped. We are no longer slaves, but whatever he does, 'Abd al-Tamm will still be 'Izz al-Qawm's son. No one will forget his origin in a village that doesn't forget. I dreamed that you would become a doctor so that we could escape together. In the capital, no one knows us. No one knows 'Izz al-Qawm. You were to be a doctor and I'd be the doctor's mother. What have you done to yourself and to me?"

She was consumed by grief when she saw the escape window closing before them.

She knew her place in Hajar Narti. She had been deceiving herself and the village as she waited for the moment of escape, when she would become the doctor's mother. For fourteen years she had been dreaming of the day she could leave the village and never return. She had promised herself to spit in the Nile and shout, "I have escaped from you. I have escaped drowning."

When Hajja Radiya withdrew her daughter from school, she thought it was a mere stumble along the path to a dream. For twenty months, she had never wavered in her ambition to placate the old woman and seek her help so she would let her daughter return to her studies. She reckoned that a school year or two's delay would only be a temporary obstacle along the path to escape. It was not unusual for escape routes to be blocked by obstacles.

But now the routes had been cut.

Hajja Radiya would never forgive her, and the mother of an illegitimate child would never go to university.

Abir had thrown away her future to live her life. She would repeat her mother's life and remain a prisoner in this village.

Perhaps the time had come for Abir to learn her method of making local wines.

Perhaps people would love "Abir Walker" as their fathers had loved "Fayit Niddu Walker."

❧

Ahmad Shigrib felt betrayed and besieged.

He didn't know whether it was his son that Abir was carrying or someone else's. He had heard several names mentioned, and his masculine pride had been hurt.

He had proposed marriage to Abir more than once. She hadn't

clearly accepted, but on the other hand, she hadn't refused.

Her second plan had been to run away. She had held this in reserve until after the failure of Rashid al-Nayir's mediation. But the pregnancy had put an end to her deception.

He couldn't believe what a fool he'd been.

She had come to him a few weeks before to tell him that she was pregnant by him.

"Marry me, and we will run away!" she had said.

Would he really have married her if what had happened hadn't happened?

"The situation has changed now, Abir!"

Where could he go to with a pregnant young girl? Could he take her back to the capital to face his mother and family and friends?

"We'll go to the capital. No one knows me there. No one will bother us there."

"You don't know Khartoum, Abir. It's a big village. Another Hajar Narti, only with electricity and paved streets. No one will show us any mercy. My family won't accept me if I marry you."

His previous assumptions were collapsing. He saw himself as almost naked, but he hastily switched to the argument that "the situation has changed" to hide his nakedness.

If it weren't for her being pregnant, I would marry her. But it would be a scandal for me to marry a young girl who gave birth after five months of marriage!

Then the tales of other people came into his head and he was afraid.

Had all those other names shared Abir with me?

Farmers and youths and old men and adolescents—had all of them shared with him her thin body, dry as a palm leaf?

"You knew."

"I didn't know there were so many."

"Is one any different from ten?"

"There's a difference."

"What's the difference?"

He shuddered and didn't know how to answer. He repeated, in a defeated tone, "There's a difference."

She left him as coldly as she had come.

She left him to the people's tongues and mockery. Whenever they saw him, they smiled and joked with him about the young girl being pregnant. No one showed anger toward him. His difficult situation was just a joke for them, for he hadn't violated any family honor, merely made pregnant a young girl descended from slaves.

Suleiman al-Hawati laughed. "This is how slave girls have been accustomed to behave since God created the world," he told him.

Despite that, he felt besieged. He wished people would forget, then he could forget. He could do without all this. He had followed his desires and had turned himself into a good story. There was no doubt the girl was a witch. She had tempted him with something that was not human. He would not have acted like that if he had been rational. It was her fault and her crime. He was an innocent victim who had been duped and led into a trap over which he had no control. Taking refuge in that innocent explanation, he sighed contentedly.

People would forget and he would forget.

There was nothing to fear.

As for the girl… let her pay the price for her adultery and seductiveness.

❦

Fayit Niddu went out, avoiding the scandal so far as she could. She passed along the deserted lanes at sunrise, making her way to Muhammad Said's house.

She was bearing her humiliation and defeat in a final attempt at mediation. Perhaps there were still miracles to come. One last miracle. A small miracle for her sake wouldn't break the laws of the earth or upset the arrangement of the heavens.

One miracle for my sake for the Messenger of God and the righteous saints.

She walked fearfully, borne along by trepidation and paralyzed by apprehension.

She went into her masters' house and found the revered sheikh on his prayer mat beside the door. She stood humbly before him.

"Good morning, Hajj!"

He raised his head to look at her, the loving slave who was nearly the same age as him. They had lived their whole lives together in one house, where she had been born. Her mother, 'Izz al-Qawm, had protected him and looked after him as a child. Fayit Niddu had been his constant companion. He had no sisters, so for a time he counted her as a sister. He quickly dropped the beads of his rosary.

"Good morning, dear sister!"

She knelt beside him.

"I've come to you to ask you to mediate with my mother, Hajj!"

She made him nervous but his face did not change.

"What do you want?"

"My daughter, Hajj!"

"That is a serious matter you are asking."

"If it is serious, your mediation is more serious."

"Niddu, this is a matter in which the Hajja will not accept mediation."

"I am only asking for her consent. I will kiss the ground under her feet if she will allow the girl to go back to school."

"God's command is final, my sister!"

"I swear by the might of the deceased, Hajj Bashir and my mother, 'Izz al-Qawm."

"God's command is final."

She said nothing and her tears flowed, but Muhammad Said left her to her sorrow. He could do nothing to help her. The Nile would dry up before the fire in Radiya's heart cooled for the girl. No one would dare to argue with her in this matter after the scandal of Abir's pregnancy. Not her husband, Muhammad Said, not even the old al-Nayir if he rose from his grave.

Fayit Niddu would come to know that now. Hajja Radiya left the kitchen followed by a Bedouin carrying the morning tea utensils.

The old woman frowned when she saw Fayit al-Niddu kneeling beside the sheikh.

She mumbled, just audibly, "Good morning!"

Fayit Niddu erupted into tears. She clung to the woman, having made up her mind to pour out all the fervent pleas she possessed at her feet.

"By God and the Prophet of God, forgive her, Hajja!"

Radiya snatched her hand away from the distraught mother.

"Neither you nor your daughter know God or His Prophet. Or your mother, or your ancestors. A cursed origin and a filthy lineage!"

"Hajja, your judgment on me is final and whatever you say about me I will accept. But forgive the girl."

"I wouldn't be my father's daughter if I did that!"

"Kill me and forgive her!"

"You deserve it. She only did what you did."

Radiya was burning with hatred. There was no room in her heart for mercy. She resisted Fayit Niddu's pleas. She was a solid rock that would not be softened. May God have mercy on Sukaina, daughter of al-Badri. There was no loving heart in this village except for hers.

Muhammad Said got up to go to his seat under the acacia tree in front of the house and Fayit Niddu followed him, broken hearted. Radiya poured tea for him. Two spoonfuls of sugar and he indicated that was enough. "Drink your tea, Niddu!" he begged her.

She thanked him with an inaudible mutter. "It's years since we drank tea together. Perhaps thirty years or more. I don't remember any longer," he said.

She wished she was brave enough to say to him, "I don't remember any companionship at that time."

She moved her lips but the words came out as, "They were good years, and you were the best of brothers."

Radiya chided her, "Is there anything else, apart from your daughter, the bastard, and what is in her belly?"

Muhammad Said protested in embarrassment, "That's not right, Hajja!"

"It's not right that your brother, who's coming now, should arrive and find this servant talking to you as if she were a free woman."

Muhammad Said turned and saw Rashid coming for his appointment with him. His heart froze.

What was this difficult morning?

He pointed to Fayit Niddu.

"Sorry, Niddu. Rashid and I are having a private conversation."

She nodded her head sorrowfully. "Come back at another time," he told her. "I'd love to drink coffee with you and talk as we used to when we were young. I've lost Bashir and I no longer have anyone to talk to."

Radiya gave him a threatening look, and he indicated he was busy by looking at Rashid as he approached.

Fayit Niddu left, like the shadow of a wall as evening approaches. She passed Rashid and he gave her a cool greeting. His heart was blazing with fire. When he had seen her in the distance, he had not had a good feeling. Why should his brother call him early and find Fayit Niddu with him? Had Abir given him away? No one knew their secret, so perhaps she had exposed him to keep her own disgrace a secret. No one would criticize him if she had been another slave girl, but he was an uncle to Abir. That would mangle his reputation for a while. He would become the village gossip. The adulterer who made his niece pregnant! Oh, what a disgrace!

He sat in front of his brother and Radiya, but avoided looking at them. He wished he had listened to Abir when she hurried to him some weeks ago to tell him that she was pregnant by him. He had angered her when he denied it. He told her to go to Ahmad Shigrib to have an abortion but she had cried out in fury, "I will die before that!"

"Why do you refuse?" he asked her. "It's a pregnancy that will bring me and you nothing but trouble. Get rid of it without anyone knowing."

"And what about Shigrib? Aren't you afraid of him knowing my secret?"

"There are many secrets between you and Shigrib," he told her quietly.

"Let this be another one."

"What secrets are there between us?"

He was confused. He told her he knew. He knew the day when she had given herself to Shigrib under his brother's palm trees. Passers-by had noticed them and people had made jokes about them. And he had seen her walking off behind him to the surgery more than once.

"Why should that annoy you?"

He was ashamed to tell her that she was a slave girl so he wouldn't expect anything else from her.

The flame danced in her eyes and she went away. Now he was afraid that she might have taken vengeance on him.

But his brother saved him from his apprehension, only to push him into another chasm.

He told him why he had summoned him and he was blown away by astonishment!

✿

The stories of the night Bashir al-Nayir died are never forgotten.

Time passes with the river Nile, but the stories do not fade. They are passed on during village gatherings, one feeding another.

The village talked of the massacres of the new regime. Planes flattened Aba Island on the White Nile south of the capital. The Imam of the Ansar al-Mahdi was killed. The regime had become brutal. The officer in charge stood up and proclaimed, "The Revolution is the left. There is no room in it for the right."

They consoled the al-Badri family, who had supported the Ansar al-Mahdi, but they were afraid of the military, so feigned indifference.

They talked about Ahmad Shigrib and how he had fled. They always remembered good things about him.

They laughed about what had happened the night Bashir al-Nayir had died.

It was a winter's evening, with a frost that tore thick skins to pieces. The sad news made its way along the paths, that Hajj Bashir al-Nayir had died. The evil disease had laid him low.

People came out of their houses in astonishment, the old consoling the young. They told each other to be patient as they wept to one another.

Hajj Bashir al-Nayir had died. Let the houses slap their faces and let palm trees howl! There was no one to give comfort, no one to give comfort.

Hajj Bashir al-Nayir had died.

Muhammad Said did not try to bear it, he cried like a small child. The marks on his cheeks were filled with tears. Nur al-Sham rolled in the dust in front of his room, as Rashid fastened his turban around his waist and bellowed.

The stories on that night will not be forgotten.

From the depths of the tragedy, funny stories emerged for people to laugh at for a time.

The corpse was washed and covered in a winding sheet. People waited in the cold courtyard for the burial in the morning. Different groups stood around the blazing fire, as they tried to get warm.

The cold was eating at Suleiman al-Hawati's heart, so he slipped away to look for a warm room where he could hide. Whenever he poked his head into a room he found it crammed full of people whispering sorrowfully. He walked about the house, looking for a room where he could find refuge. There was one empty room. In the darkness he saw a black mass on a single bed. This was a room that people avoided. He walked toward the bed in the darkness. A penetrating smell filled the place. "'Abd al-Razeq?" he asked, in a whisper.

Suleiman al-Hawati swears that he heard a faint whisper that confirmed his suspicions. 'Abd al-Razeq had beaten him to the room and occupied the only bed. He worked out the direction of his head and stretched out beside him on the bed, with his feet beside his face. "Give me some space," he said, nudging the other man with his elbow.

The man didn't answer or give him any room so he nudged him again.

"'Abd al-Razeq! Give me a bit of room!"

The smell filled his nostrils. He got closer to the feet, which were stiff. It was the smell of an embalmed corpse.

"'Abd al-Razeq?"

He stretched out his hand in the darkness. The body was dry and cold. He turned over on his right side, put his hand down to touch the ground and the damp surprised and frightened him. Suleiman had seen many corpses and had not been afraid of them or the tales told about them. But he had never slept on a bed beside a corpse before. His heart skipped a beat. His hand on the floor was wet from the water used to wash the corpse. The smell of the embalming gripped him as if he was embracing it. He screamed, turned over on the ground, then crawled away in terror as he bumped along the cold earth. He screamed and screamed and screamed then opened the door of the room and rushed out, driven by terror.

The stories did not forget what he did.

People made fun of him for a time because for being both stupid and afraid.

Even Muhammad Said al-Sheikh would laugh at this story the day after the burial. He would laugh so much that his tears flowed.

The family is more important than anything.

More important than the wishes and opinion of a single man. The interests of the group define what it should love and dream of.

Rashid was caught in this trap and could not escape.

Muhammad Said told him, "We are all the same view."

He turned around to look for a way out but Hajja Radiya was standing there.

"Congratulations."

"But Hajj!" he stammered.

"Congratulations!"

Would he be led to drown and not resist? But how could he oppose his esteemed brother? They would marry him off to Nur al-Sham, the widow of his deceased brother. It was decided. He had no say in the matter now that the family had made its decision.

"She is older than me, Hajj! There are four or five years between us."

"Is that a difference of any significance? Our Master, the Prophet, married Khadija, who was twenty-five years older than him."

"I am not a prophet!"

"I seek forgiveness from God. Is there any model except for the Prophet?"

In vain did he struggle in his chains.

"I have no desire for this marriage, Hajj!"

Radiya chided him, "Does any man refuse marriage?"

"Can a man be forced into a marriage he does not want?"

Muhammad Said spoke to him more gently. "Son of my mother, this is good for you, as well as for the al-Nayir family. We will not leave the inheritance of the deceased for the al-Badri family to play with."

So you will play with me? Would they throw him into the Nile to redeem an inheritance?

"The al-Badri family will not accept this."

"Your uncles have spoken to them. They will not refuse if you ask for her."

So that was it. The interests of the two families were united against him. He had been plunged into a crisis, caught between Abir's pregnancy and a forced marriage.

Could he be saved by confessing to the marriage between him and Abir?

"My brother's wife! But I have usually thought of her as an older sister!"

"Thinking is one thing, but the facts are something different!"

There was no escape, no escape! He was suspended on the family's interests. For the sake of the inheritance, his family would do anything.

"Azhari, Bashir's son, is our son; his wealth is our wealth and his land is our land," said Radiya. "You are his uncle and closer to him than anyone. So leave the weeping to the women and settle the matter like a man."

So the woman who had been married to her cousin to complete the formalities of the 'umda was driving him now to the same fate.

*If only I were like you, Radiya! If only I had your sense of propriety
and respect for tradition. But I am weaker than you, less unrelenting. I
have no way out, there is nothing I can do.*

He visited the al-Badri household perforce, and asked for Nur
al-Sham in marriage, even though death would have been easier for
him. They made conditions and demands and he argued with them
unsuccessfully.

In a few weeks, he found himself engaged to the woman he had
for ten years thought of as a sister, as his brother's comfort and joy. And
now, they were preparing her to be his own comfort. He would sleep in
his brother's bed and inherit his wealth and his wife.

Nur al-Sham sat with him, pale as a corpse.

"I have nothing to offer you."

"We are all powerless, Rashid."

"Forgive me for my weakness."

Her face grew darker. Her eyes, which so attracted the attention of
her aunt Sukaina, were lakes of sorrow.

"May the deceased forgive us!"

He looked at her, his soul filled with misgiving. Medium height,
thin, in her mid-thirties. She wasn't pretty, but she was pleasant enough.
Older than him, and a mother, but you wouldn't turn her down. If she
hadn't been his brother's widow.

He cast his eye over her.

She was prettier than Abir, who had captivated him.

"May the deceased forgive us!"

He wandered the streets, not knowing what to do.

Abir's belly was growing larger, and with it the scandal. The time
for his wedding was approaching and he was sick at heart.

His body grew thinner and he wished he could be struck down by
the terrible disease.

Time moved on, summer approached, and with it the ghajar. But
he could not leave; he was just like Fayit Niddu, unable to save herself
and her daughter.

He asked himself whether Abir had become pregnant by him or

if she had deceived him.

His colleague Ahmad Shigrib had been weighed down by the slander and mirth of the village and had left. He had visited Muhammad Said and told him that he had been forced to resign. He would go back to the capital. Communism was no longer a crime, and the whole country was singing for the October star and Bolshevism and fighting the forces of reaction. Perhaps he would find a place there. Perhaps he would forget Abir and her pregnancy and their times together. He would flee to cure himself of the sorcery and the sorceress.

Ahmad Shigrib would go back to his family, but how would Rashid escape from his family?

His roots were here, and his life was here. He was born in Hajar Narti, and here was his family, killing him in Hajar Narti. His life and his death were both here.

He would submit to his fate. He would leave himself to the waves of the River Nile to carry him wherever they wanted.

Let them marry him off. Nothing mattered.

It was as if Abir's pregnancy was hurried because of him.

He finished his days without delaying. His death throes came in their time as Mahjoub had foreseen.

The world clouded over in Fayit Niddu's eyes when the labor pains came to her daughter. Fayit Niddu wished her grandson could be born and set them all free, but he refused. The girl went into labor and she cried out as her waters broke. Then it was over, like a rush of wind. She didn't suffer like other pregnant women. As if he was in a hurry to arrive, it was all over. The wrinkled infant cried in the arms of his grandmother, covered in blood, as sweat flowed over his mother's thin body.

Groups of women came together out of politeness and curiosity to bless him.

"May our Lord preserve him."

"Praise God for his mother's health."

"May Gabriel's wings cover him."

Fayit Niddu looked at him. She remembered her own baby girl lying wrinkled in her arms. One illegitimate birth leading to another. A family tree that had not known marriage since the caravan of slaves brought 'Izz al-Qawm's mother.

How insubstantial we are on this earth.

It gives us no honor.

Its men amuse themselves with us and we suffer.

Who is your father, weepy one?

She pushed him toward Abir and she gave him her breast, tiny as a lemon.

"Blessings for your health, my daughter!"

Was this a look of happiness in Abir's eyes?

Fayit Niddu could not tell her what she did not know. "Forgive me!" she whispered.

Abir paid no attention. She looked at her child, glowing.

When he sucked on her nipples a feeling of the joy of creation passed through her. This infant was part of her, like a missing piece of her soul coming back to its place. Lying there covered in sweat, she looked like a wise, mature lady. The quick birth had given her a glow and seemed to have lit her up.

Then Radiya jumped up like a piece of bad news.

The old woman, who could not forgive!

Fayit Niddu had begged God for her to either forget or forgive or die, but heaven did not answer the slave. Hajja Radiya came like a judgment that could not be rejected. As she walked, followed by the ghajari, her shadow on the ground was loud with pride. She had made up her mind about what should be, and there was no going back on it.

Years ago, she had relented, given in to various people's appeals, and left Fayit Niddu to have her baby girl and come back to the village. And here she was, an evil plant generating more evil. She would not relent this time. She would burn Abir and her mother's hearts as they had burned her own heart.

She felt consumed by fire when someone went against something she believed in. She blazed inside and was filled with anger. She rushed into the fight with no possibility of a truce, as if she were a cat defending its kittens.

Her husband often implored her to modify her nature.

"Hajja, leave people to their maker!" But she wouldn't accept anything less than the imposition of her will in its entirety.

"Our traditions, Sheikh Muhammad! Tradition is everything! There is no room for folly or bad manners. If we leave people to indulge in filth, what will we have left?"

"The world is changing, Hajja. People are free. No one does what you do."

"I only do for them what they are too lazy to do themselves. I am simply protecting my people's heritage from any kind of damage."

He knew she was searching for meaning in her long submission to her family. She was being killed by adhering to something that did not give value to her life. If she didn't fight in defense of her ancestors' heritage, what had she given her life for, why had she submitted herself to them? Her submission had no value unless others were subject to her. And to that end, she would burn the hearts of Fayit Niddu and Abir.

Fayit Niddu had haggled some weeks before about what she wanted. The child in exchange for allowing Abir to go back to school.

That had seemed a reasonable solution at the time in the eyes of Fayit Niddu. Abir would be free of the child and would go back to school. With a certain amount of effort, she would forget what had happened. Fayit Niddu knew that several free women had given birth in the village as a result of passing affairs, then abandoned the child and married. She knew women in the al-Nayir family who had done that, and they and everyone else had forgotten it. Abir's life would heal and she would go to university. She would become a doctor and they would escape to the capital. That was a price she could pay.

But when she saw the child her heart almost burst into song. Abir's happiness opened her eyes and she realized the enormity of what she had done.

She wished Radiya would forget what they had agreed upon. She wished she would forgive or die. But she did not forget, or forgive, or die.

She came, as the time always comes.

Fayit Niddu took the child from the breast of her daughter. Abir was afraid and rushed to try to snatch it. But Hajja Radiya seized it by force. "Forgive me!" Fayit Niddu whispered.

Radiya took hold of him in disgust, Abir screamed, and Fayit Niddu shed tears. The women who had gathered out of courtesy and curiosity were horror-struck.

The old woman handed the child to her ghajari companion.

Salih the ghajari was tall, with an enormous belly that protruded in front of him. His eyes were colored like those of most ghajar and his skin was light, encrusted with dirt.

"Here is what I promised you," she said in a thick, drawn-out voice.

"God bless you, Hajja!"

Abir leaped on him and Radiya pushed her away. She fell to the ground, uttering imprecations. For the first time, her voice could be heard out loud, animated by the fire in her heart.

Her mother held her, cuddling her and crying with her. "Forgive me, Abir. Abandoning children is hard but your mother is weak."

Radiya and Salih the ghajari took the child away, leaving Abir to her misery.

That afternoon, the ghajar left Hajar Narti and did not come back.

By her gift, Radiya had fulfilled al-Afiya's promise to Bahiya's family. She had also spared the al-Badri family the ghajar descending on their land to agree to the marriage of Nur al-Sham to Rashid.

With one stroke, the old woman had achieved several aims.

And through a child that she could not accept she had imposed what she wanted.

That was her happiest day.

❧

We two are alone. We have no one.

Fayit Niddu woke as the sun crept into the room.

She was worn out from staying awake crying beside Abir's bed, then slept until the sun was high in the dome of the sky. She was kneeling on the ground, her head resting on the empty bed.

She sprung up in alarm. Where was the girl?

She ran into the courtyard consumed by terror, then went out through the tumbledown part of the rear wall. She called loudly to Abir. The girl wasn't doing her business in the open space behind the house. Her mother came back into the courtyard and back into the room again. She searched the empty bed as though her daughter might be hiding inside it.

Exhausted from finding nothing, she ran into Muhammad Said's house, and burst in on Hajja Radiya like a hurricane.

"Where is my daughter?"

Radiya glowered.

"Good morning. Why should your daughter be with us?"

Fayit Niddu rushed frantically around the sheikh's house, calling her daughter. She went into every room, even surprising Muhammad Said in his hideaway. Nothing stopped her.

The household all collected around her: the district sheikh Muhammad Said, the slave girls and the Bedouin girls, but not Radiya, who retreated into a corner, muttering, "Where else would the bastard go? She'll be with her cursed mates."

They tried to calm Fayit Niddu. But her heart was ablaze and would not be placated.

The news made its way from the sheikh's house and caught up with everyone. They followed it until the weeping Fayit Niddu came to the courtyard of Muhammad Said's house.

More and more people collected around her to offer their reassurances.

"Everything will be alright, Fayit Niddu, God willing!"

"Don't think the worst too quickly!"

"It's a small village. Where could she go? We'll find her."

'Abd al-Razeq appeared from among the crowd, and Muhammad Said ordered him to follow the trail.

'Abd al-Razeq took Fayit Niddu by the hand, stood her up, and walked with her, crowds following. Hajja Radiya stayed behind in her kitchen, along with her servants who obeyed her.

"Disaster take her!" the old woman thundered. "A bastard of a girl. A devil, born of devils."

From Fayit Niddu's courtyard, 'Abd al-Razeq followed the trail of the barefoot girl, bending low as he did so. The crowd followed behind him, exchanging comments.

"He's found the track!"

"She left the house."

"She passed by the mosque."

'Abd al-Razeq walked down, following the track until the ground changed. As the sand disappeared, black, fertile soil took its place. They passed under the palm trees, pursued by the trees' curiosity. Birds flew over them and the smell of guavas hit them. The barefoot tracks headed steadily to the east. Rashid walked in the middle of the crowd, helping his brother Muhammad Said. His heart was trembling. They passed the remains of the camp of the ghajar who had left yesterday. People whispered to one another.

"Have the ghajar gone?"

"Don't you know what happened?"

"What's the story?"

The account of what Hajja Radiya had done made its way among them from lip to lip. They marveled, sought refuge in God, and made no further comment.

The tracks went on to their destiny. A clear trail that left its marks on the earth as it headed for the jetty.

The crowd, drawn by courtesy and curiosity, were struck dumb.

'Abd al-Razeq bent lower over the ground. He walked on until the tracks ended.

He stood on the bank of the Nile and looked at the waves beneath him.

He swallowed hard and put his two hands on his waist.

"There is no power or might save in God!"

He turned toward those following him. His eyes were on Fayit Niddu's eyes. His face was filled with sorrow. The palm trees took fright when Fayit Niddu's scream rang out from within her blazing body.

"Abir!"

Three days later, Suleiman al-Hawati saw Fatima, the girl's mother, hurrying along the bank of the Nile, heading north.

Someone had told her that the corpse of a drowned girl had appeared, so she had gone out to look for it, in case it was Su'ad.

POSTSCRIPT

- **Fayit Niddu** still lives in Hajar Narti and is nearly a hundred years old. Rashid al-Nayir and his wife Nur al-Sham take care of her.

- After the abolition of the family administrative system, the **al-Nayir family** no longer enjoys any authority, but the title of 'umda is still passed down among them.

- **The military regime** remained in power for sixteen years until April 1985. It carried out several massacres. It bombed Aba Island and killed about 10,000 of the Ansar al-Mahdi, in addition to liquidating several leaders of the Communist Party. It abandoned its leftist philosophy, moved to the right, proclaimed government by Islamic law, and carried out executions for apostasy.

  There are no exact statistics for the number of people killed during those sixteen years.

- **Hajja Radiya** moved to the capital after the death of her husband, Muhammad Said. She lived with one of her sons and survived for a long time but went blind at the end of her life.

- **Ahmad Shigrib** was imprisoned for a time after Communists had been tortured by the regime. He then secured a post in Saudi Arabia and moved there at the end of the 1970s.

- **Nur al-Sham** had two sons by Rashid. The elder was called Bashir, after his late uncle.

- **Fatima**, the girl's mother, still appears, waiting for Su'ad's corpse.